ENDORSEMENTS

PRAISE FOR THE AUTHOR

"David Agranoff is a razor sharp writer, a storyteller with hard rock pacing, a magician of ideas ... An idealist in hell." — John Shirley, cyberpunk legend and screenwriter of *The Crow*

"A wonderful new voice" — Jeremy Robert Johnson, author of *The Loop*

"Agranoff brings an artist's eye and activist's fist to these chilling reports from our war on the natural world." — Cody Goodfellow, author of *Unamerica*

"I've been a big fan of David Agranoff since his first novel *'The Vegan Revolution... with* Zombies' came out a few years ago through Eraserhead. The thing that always attracted me to Agranoff was his punk rock ethos, one he refuses to shed—a straight-edger with a penchant for violence and smart humor, which permeated in his fiction. He was always one of the bizarre writers I wanted to be myself." — Chris Kelso, author of *I Dream Of Mirrors* and *Voidheads*

PRAISE FOR THE LAST NIGHT TO KILL NAZIS

"At the beginning of *The Last Night to Kill Nazis*, David Agranoff lights a fuse that burns with perfectly-timed suspense to an explosive resolution. This mash-up of World War II thriller and vampire horror is exciting and authentic; like peanut butter and chocolate, it shouldn't work, but it does. I loved it!" — Lisa Morton, six-time Bram Stoker Award winner

"*The Last Night to Kill Nazis* is solid storytelling packed with real history and—if you are of the mindset that evil deserves to be punished—a whole hell of a lot of bloody, gratifying fun." — Alma Katsu, author of *The Wehrwolf*

"A brutal, bloody rampage; Agranoff has created great characters and daring storytelling. I guarantee you have never had so much fun seeing Nazis meeting their gruesome fates." — Tim Lebbon, author of *The Silence* and *The Last Storm*

"*The Last Night to Kill Nazis* is a glorious exploration of culpability and trauma. A blood-soaked thrill ride bursting with frenetic energy that recalls the finest of exploitation and action films. David Agranoff looks at the horrors of the second World War with unflinching honesty, exploring a culpability that few other writers dare to. This is a book that balances exceptional depth with absolute fun and terrific characters. Come for Nazis dying horribly, and stay for the fantastic writing." — Zachary Rosenberg, author of *Hungers As Old As This Land* and *The Long Shalom*

PRAISE FOR PUNK ROCK GHOST STORY

"*Punk Rock Ghost Story* is a beautiful journey back-in-time to the early years of American hardcore punk. It's part horror story and part nostalgic road trip." — Jack Bantry, Splatterpunk Zine

PRAISE FOR THE VEGAN REVOLUTION... WITH ZOMBIES

"*Vegan Revolution... with Zombies* is my kind of zombie apocalypse. A perfect blend of horror, humor and animal activism. Destined to become a favorite among zombie fans and vegans alike." — Gina Ranalli, author of *House of Fallen Trees*

PRAISE FOR AMAZING PUNK STORIES

"With zombies, post-apocalyptic mayhem, ferocious creatures, and more, *Amazing Punk Stories* has plenty of punk rock soaked pulp action. Each story is clever and well written, offering enough great ideas to keep you entertained." — Horror Undergound

DAVID AGRANOFF
PEOPLE'S PARK

All rights reserved. No part of this book may be used or reproduced, stored in a retrieval system, or transmitted in any form or by any means, electronic, mechanical, photocopying, recording, scanning, or otherwise, without written permission from the publisher except in the case of brief quotations embodied in critical articles and reviews. Permission for wider usage of this material can be obtained through Quoir by emailing permission@quoir.com.

This is a work of fiction. The characters, places, and incidents portrayed, and the names used herein are fictitious or used in a fictitious manner. Any resemblance to the name, character, or history of any person, living or dead, is coincidental and unintentional. Product names used herein are not an endorsement of this work by the produce name owners.

Copyright © 2024 by David Agranoff
First Edition

Cover Design by Matthew J. Distefano & Rafael Polendo (polendo.net)
Interior Layout by Matthew J. Distefano

ISBN 978-1-957007-94-6

QUOIR

Published by Quoir
Chico, California
www.quoir.com

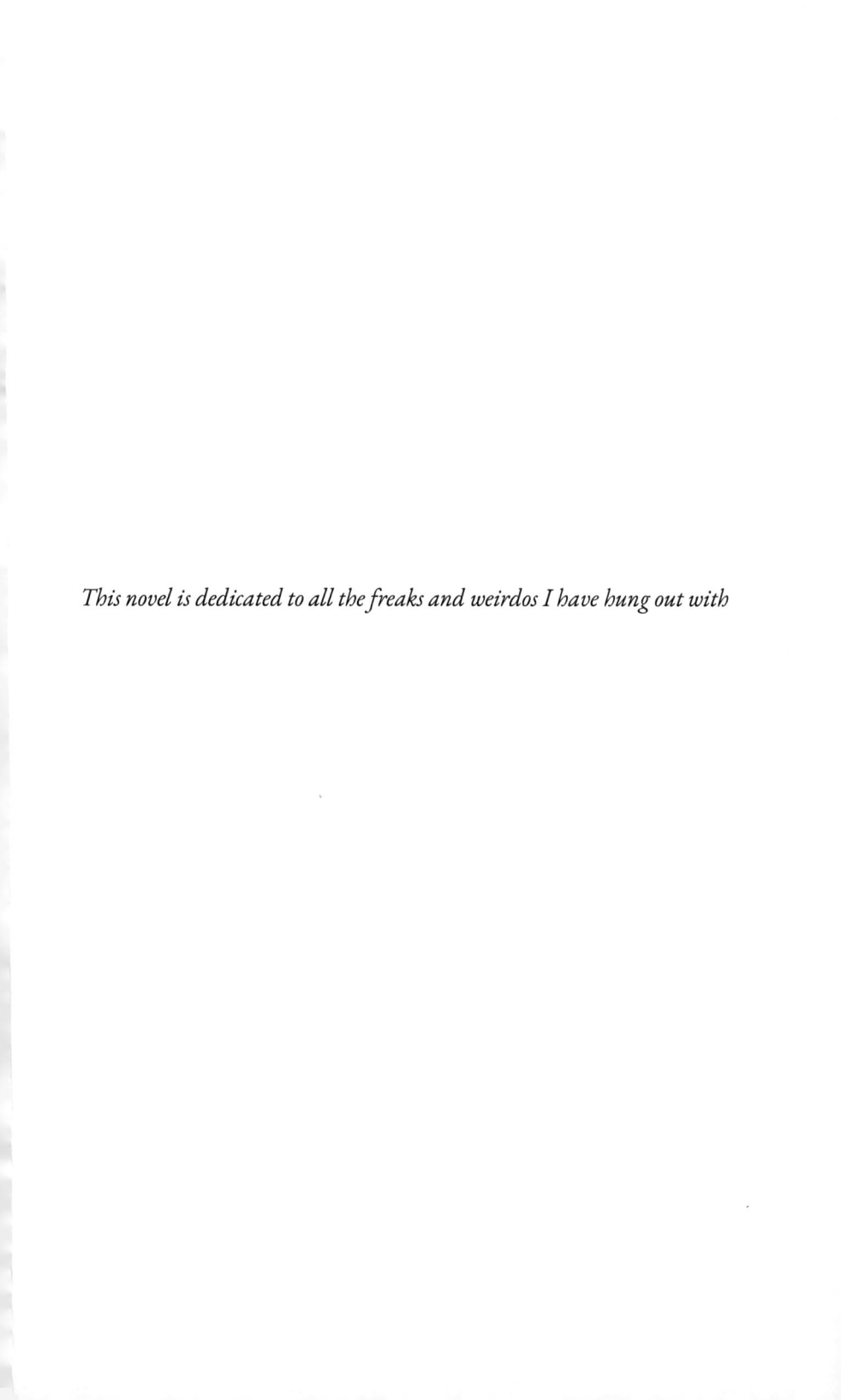

This novel is dedicated to all the freaks and weirdos I have hung out with

"You say the dream and the world are two separate things, and that is because you have yet to awaken from the dream. Chung Chou once dreamed he was a butterfly, and upon waking he could not tell if he was the butterfly dreaming he was Chung Chou."

— **The Nine Cloud Dream by Kim Man-Jung**

"Civilization's dying and no one's realizing. The position of hate stuck inside the gun Civilization's crying And I won't try to deny it. We got a problem son, something's gotta be done"

— **Zero Boys**

PROLOGUE

Bloomington Indiana
December 28th, 1969, 12:36 AM

She looked at more than a billion stars and sighed. The focus was just slightly off since she last looked. It was amazing that with a few small pieces of glass they could see the whole universe.

"It moved, didn't it?" Freddy asked. He sounded frustrated, but even though her view of the cluster of stars was out of focus, she was happy. They had the old observatory all to themselves. Other women might not find this romantic, but Catherine did.

He was nervous pointing out the obvious. The earth was always moving and had moved enough that they had lost their view on the wild duck cluster; a neighborhood of stars roughly 57 light-years away that crowded almost 3,000 suns together. Even in the view of such wonder her Sugar-Bear was still nervous around her.

"Could you please?" Catherine smiled from the top of the rolling ladder. She looked in the eyepiece of the telescope that reached up through the open roof into the winter night. This scope had been the centerpiece of Kirkwood Observatory for sixty years now. She felt him push the telescope slightly and then roll the ladder.

"Just a little more Sugar."

He groaned at her favorite nickname for him but he knew his moves in this dance well. The pinpricks of light that traveled many millions of miles came into tight focus.

"How does it look?"

Vivid, beautiful. Words always failed her when seeing the universe working at such large scales.

"See for yourself," she said.

He climbed up the ladder as she slid past to give him the space and took a second to smile at him. It was the first Christmas she had spent away from home. They were one semester short of earning their Astronomy degrees from Indiana University. She had stayed in Bloomington over the summer to catch up to him while he worked extra shifts at a refrigerator plant. She had skipped the demonstrations in Dunn Meadow for the first time since she was a sophomore.

Her mother didn't like Freddy, didn't like that he and his mother were estranged, but Catherine didn't want him to spend the holiday alone. Plus, she knew he had been carrying a ring around for weeks and she was waiting for him to pop the question. The thing was her Sugar-Bear was a scientist and not a romantic. He was also filled with anxiety and thought any fight over dishes or what to eat was the end. His mother, who died just a year before he started IU, had constantly instilled fear in him.

"How's it look; the magic of stars being born and dancing together?" she asked.

"Crushing gravity between stars," his eyes glued to the eyepiece. "The power is destructive. It's unlikely any of these stars host life."

"Yep, still magical," she whispered. They bonded over their love of the night sky, but they met chasing justice. She had seen him lined up for the protest bus and recognized his face from the astronomy department. He was as awkward as it got, with bushy hair, bottleneck glasses and jeans that seemed to be hiding any kind of ass. He wasn't much to look at, with a hairline that was already receding and skin that was vampire white, but he was into space and was ready to shout down Nixon, so she sat next to him on the bus.

He turned to sit at the top of the ladder and snapped his fingers. She knew what he wanted. She passed him the notebook they bought the year before. His roommate had a double major in weed and SDS so his side of the room was an abandoned mess. The first night they spent together was in his room. The idea was to make a list of stars they wanted to see together.

The Kirkwood Observatory was a dinosaur replaced by a newer facility thirty miles north in a darker site. But this old building was on Campus just outside of the downtown strip and a short walk from their dorms. So they checked out the keys and spent most nights there when the weather was good.

Fred checked off another item from their list. They had forty left of the two-hundred-and-thirty-night sky objects they wanted to see together. She waited for the high five that was a part of this ritual. He was not celebrating. She knew he had the ring in his pocket. She thought choosing to stay on the empty campus with him over Christmas break would be encouragement enough, but the ring stayed in his pocket. The sadness on his face told her not to expect anything tonight.

"What's wrong?" She asked.

"Christmas offensive by the North."

She understood. He was obsessed with news out of Southeast Asia. His younger brother lacked his good grades and couldn't defer. He wasn't much for letters, and her Sugar assumed every battle was the one to take out the other family he had left. He had been holding on to the news all night.

"There was a cross burning north of town," he added.

As progressive as many of the students were, and as hard as they pushed Bloomington to change, they lived in a racist state. Segregation was not legal but economically enforced, and the Klan in the small towns around the University didn't like the growing radical black student unions. Fred followed the movements of the Klan locally and was convinced it was only a matter of time before they attacked.

Catherine took his hand into hers. She knew that nothing she said made him feel better.

"Hey we got three," she pointed at the new checkmarks in their personal star catalog. "How about a beer?"

He didn't smile; didn't budge an inch. When Catherine had gotten their graduation dates to match they had discussed looking for Astronomy gigs they could take together. Catherine had made the mistake of mentioning school systems. She wanted children. He feared unending drafts and body counts, race riots and red buttons with the ability to kill everyone in a matter of minutes. She wondered if his fear to bring children into this world may be the reason the ring was still in his pocket.

He smiled. She suspected he was faking but one reason she loved him was the way his eyes beheld her. He gazed into the light time traveling around the curves of space and he marveled at her. Her freckles, her blue eyes, and shoulder-length hair. She felt pretty when he looked at her. *Get out the damn ring you moron*, was all she kept thinking.

She got. "Yeah, Beer."

He waited by the steps to the building as she turned the lock. He kicked the light snow and watched his breath rise in the cold night air.

"Nick's?" she asked. He shrugged his shoulders. She hooked his arms and got as close as she could to him. They only had two blocks to walk but it was cold enough to make that uncomfortable. She brushed up against his leg and felt the bump of the ring box. He had to know that she knew.

Nick's Tavern on Kirkwood Avenue was the only one of the bars open over the break. Normally it would be packed, and it would not be the bar they would choose. A destination for frat boys, it was just a block from the western edge of campus.

Kirkwood stretched through downtown Bloomington, away from campus, and became 5th Avenue. Closer to campus it was named after the astronomer who founded their department. When school was in session the street would have traffic, even at this late hour.

The street was home to several bars and restaurants and the marquee for the Von Lee movie theater lit the night in its flashing neon glow. Besides the theater, the first block west of campus was filled with stores that catered to students; record shops, incense, jewelry, and the controversial Black Market, a store that sold Afrocentric books and had become an organizing center for radical black students.

On this late December night, Kirkwood was quiet. The snow had melted in the roads and the clear skies left a bitterly cold night. She hooked her man's arm as they walked past the movie theater. It was closed and all the lights were out inside except the glow of empty popcorn machine. *2001: A Space Odyssey* was still playing. He had loved it and left the theater insisting they wait up until morning when they could get a look at Jupiter. She stopped to stare at the poster with him. They both talked about seeing it again.

"Hey Cath," he blocked the poster and turned to her. He was smiling with an uncharacteristically goofy smile. "I'm nervous. Just give me a second..."

She couldn't understand why he chose this moment, this spot. But she prepared herself to say yes. He lowered himself to one knee. When he did, she saw a car creeping slowly up the street over his shoulder. She almost didn't see the Buick in darkness, rolling without lights as it pulled up across from The Black Market.

She locked eyes with her Sugar Bear. He nervously looked away. She tried to follow his eyes and ended up looking past him.

"Uh, so you know I love you, and I think you love me," he said.

The Buick stopped in the left lane. A tall white man jumped out of the far side of the car holding a bottle. Even at this distance, Catherine understood what she was seeing. A sock was hanging from it. The man dangled a zippo under it.

She grabbed her Sugar and pulled. He turned in time to see the man throw the bottle and watched the flame streak towards the store window.

Catherine stumbled back as the tall white man jumped back in the Buick. The wheels spun on the wet pavement as it tore out.

"Go back to Africa!" A voice yelled from the car.

Catherine laid flat on the ground for a moment and reached out for her man. He was not beside her. She looked up and saw that he was staring at the glow of the fire. She stood up and walked up behind him slowly.

"Sweetie?"

He didn't respond as he just stared in the fire. The store was quickly burning.

"Sweetie come on we have to find a phone get help or it's gonna burn down."

He seemed frozen in place. Catherine pulled as hard as she could but he wouldn't budge. He stayed and watched as she ran to the payphone near the theater.

It would be months before she heard his voice again.

CHAPTER ONE

Bloomington Indiana
June 4th, 1989

JUSTIN RAN THROUGH THE woods for the last time. He could hear Ray's footsteps behind him. They had run this stretch of woods directly behind his house more times than he could count. It had been a stand-in for the forest of Endor, Middle Earth and many exotic jungles explored by their takes on Indiana Jones.

They knew every vine, every fallen tree, every patch of green and they had worn down their own personal trails to the creek where they had just enough water to skip rocks.

"I'll beat you!" Ray yelled. They were too old to pretend at this point but they wanted one last run of the woods together. Justin looked through the canopy of trees that put a green veil up over the two-story home that he had lived in as long as he could remember. He didn't have a shred of memory about their first house, but they had been in this house since he could walk, and they had played in these woods since they met in kindergarten.

"Hey," his cousin Nate called from the backyard. He was starting seventh grade next year and they were starting eighth. He and his aunt drove down from Chicago to help them move out of the house, and he thought being from Chicago made him super cool. He was half a foot shorter, had shaved his head, and wore huge boots.

Since he showed up this summer, he insisted they call him Smiley. All that made him sound cool to them, but he was still afraid to come into the woods.

"Hey! Fuck this I'm going inside!" Smiley yelled.

Justin knew his mother would give him a hard time about it later. His mother and Auntie Jules wanted the boys to be better friends than they were, but if Smiley didn't want to come into the woods that was his problem.

Ray pulled ahead in the recently declared race to the creek, leaping over a fallen tree that had been their cover in many laser battles with the galactic empire. Justin ran harder but Ray jumped on to the pile of rocks that were in a dry section of the creek bed first.

The stream had narrowed to a super-thin point before the part they called the lake. The creek was bent in just the right spot so water collected in a small pool that, when they were smaller, it seemed enormous. They searched for skipping rocks.

"I'm gonna miss your house," said Ray. His voice was a little more Indiana than his with a twang that changed *wash* to *wersh*. Both his parents were salt-of-the-earth Hoosiers, whereas Justin's parents grew up on the northside of Chicago.

"Why can't you just stay?"

Justin didn't want to talk about it. He had asked his mother the same thing a thousand times. She said the house was too big for just the two of them. He had told Ray before.

Justin found a smooth rock and chucked it. It bounced across the water twice. He lifted his arms like he was signaling a field goal.

"Smiley said you're getting a TV in your room at the new house," Ray said.

Justin nodded.

Ray plopped a rock without a skip. "My folks ain't ever gonna let me have a TV in my bedroom."

Justin didn't want the TV, not if the price was losing the house. It wasn't just the woods they were losing. They were losing the basketball hoop on top of the garage that they only had for a year. They had just graduated from the laundry basket with a hole cut in the bottom that they had tied to the staircase in the basement. His Dad replaced the basket a few times, tying it higher to the banister on the stairs that rose out of the basement as he and his friends grew. Once they put the real deal outside, he and his dad spent hours working on his jump shot.

"Juuuuuustin!" His Mom's voice echoed through the woods. His Dad used to do that; his voice carried further. He would never hear his voice again.

"Come on," Justin waved his friend towards the house. They walked most of the path in silence.

"Shit," Ray walked and talked. "Kinda wish I was gettin' a new house."

"I like your house."

"Our house sucks, we don't even have cable."

"So, you got the cemetery and the bike hill," Justin said as they came out of the woods. The cemetery was one of the oldest in the county with people born in the 1800s buried there. The bike hill was 15% grade that was like a roller coaster for their bikes. Ray's parents told them they had to walk down the hill but that was crazy. They went super fast down that hill and ended up at the lake where they would swim.

Smiley sat on the swing set with his Walkman on. He pulled his headphones off and some loud rock blared out louder than the headphones were designed to handle.

"What the hell you dorks do out there?" Smiley looked out to the woods.

"I don't know, skip rocks, swing on vines," Justin shrugged.

"Cool," Smiley rolled his eyes. When they were younger and he was still going by Nate his cousin used to follow him around like a puppy dog. He and Auntie Jules would come down for Christmas most years, long weekends but Smiley was always afraid of the woods. He stood there with the blare from his tiny foam-covered speakers still sounding crazy.

"What is that fucking noise? asked Ray

"The Dead Kennedys."

"The what?" Justin didn't know what any of it meant.

"Punk rock dude."

"Well, it sounds fuckin' crazy to me," Ray said walking in the back door of the house.

His mother came out on the porch and snapped her fingers. "Go straight to the car we're late."

"Yes Ma'am," Ray gave Justin's mother a goofy smile. Justin knew all his friends thought his mother was pretty. Her long red hair was not nearly as striking as her bright green eyes. They were just his mother's eyes, but his whole life he heard people telling her how pretty they were. She was in shorts; she was covered in sweat her hair awkwardly stuffed in an Indiana University baseball hat.

"You OK sweetheart?"

She was worried about him, and he shook his head. It didn't occur to his thirteen-year mind that he should ask her if she was okay. She was the one that had to become a single parent to a teenager overnight, to reset their whole lives. Nope, he just thought about himself and how he didn't want to move.

"I don't wanna go."

Nicolette Morgan, Nikki to her close friends had been through so much in the last two months. It seemed to Justin that all she wanted to do was forget his father. She changed the subject whenever he brought him up.

"Auntie Jules is waiting," With that, his mother disappeared into the house.

Justin looked up at his home as he walked around to the front. The U-Haul was parked towards the back of the drive-way behind the official three-point line his father had declared, which was just a small crack that ran across most of the pavement. His mother was already in the driver's seat. Justin took one last look up to see the window to his room. The new family was moving into the house pretty soon. The boy taking his room asked if he could keep his Empire Strikes Back curtains. At the time it seemed like kiddie thing to want to keep so he agreed. Now he wanted to run up there and save his curtains.

"Justin? Ray?" Auntie Jules came out the front door and Ray was behind her the last one in the house. His Aunt was his mother's rock and roll sister who his friend Jonah called his Auntie Benatar. Her blond roots showed through sometimes but her hair was died black and she smelled like an ashtray even though she tried never to smoke in front of them.

"Left my hat," Ray shook his Cubs hat as he jumped in Auntie Jules' blue station wagon. Smiley was softly banging his head to his music. Justin was last in as the boys filled up the back seat. A box with a lamp was riding shotgun.

"Seat belts!" Auntie Jules waved at her older sister. The U-Haul pulled out first. They were not too far down the road in a stretch of farmland turned to sprawl when they saw Emily.

Emily lived in their neighborhood and was the first girl Justin ever noticed was pretty. She had long blond hair and bright blue eyes. That wasn't the best part. She was cool and liked to play Star Wars when they were younger. She didn't want to be Princess Leia ever, she always thought she should be Luke while the rest of them fought over who would be Han Solo. She was holding a Basketball her father and older brother were shooting hoops with her.

She waved and it made Justin feel awful. He wasn't even sure why. They hadn't talked in years, but she always waved, she was even prettier now.

Smiley dropped his headphones to his shoulder and stopped his tape with a snap. "Who's that?"

They were past her before Ray responded. "Emily McRoberts."

"She's a babe and she is wearing a Minor Threat shirt."

"Minor what?" Justin asked.

"They're a band," Smiley shook his head. "Don't you know nothing?"

Auntie Jules scoffed. "You're still a child what do you know about babes?"

"Ma, I'm going to be thirteen…"

"In six months, plenty of time for girls when you get older."

Justin wasn't interested in listening to this argument again. Smiley was a goofy-looking kid, giant lips that gave him his nickname with his older friends. He wore combat books and a flight jacket he almost never took off. He hung out with his older kids in the city. Justin didn't know how that happened but his cousin thought he was a grown-up.

"She's fine, you gotta introduce me," Smiley smacked Ray lightly.

"Don't matter none, she is moving…"

Justin was surprised, but he moved so he wasn't sure why he would be.

"Not just in town she is moving to California."

That hurt. He expected to see her at middle school next year. Even though they didn't talk he passed her locker every day on the way to Social Studies last year. She waved when she saw him. It was more change. Everything was changing. Ever since they lost Dad it seemed like nothing was staying the same. Justin leaned his head against the window. He felt like crying. It wasn't the Emily news, it shouldn't matter. It wasn't moving out of the house, or even losing his dad. It was all of it. Sometimes he was sad, sometimes he was angry. He didn't know how to express those feelings so it just ate at him under the surface.

He just needed to make it to the new house where his mother promised him a surprise.

CHAPTER TWO

Nikki pulled the U-haul up into the garage of their new house. It was built into a hill and the two-car garage opened into the basement. The house only had two bedrooms and a small space for her office; she was going to have work from home more now that she was alone. It was not the nicest house, it had scuffed up hardwood floors where she wanted to have carpets, the yard was an overgrown mess that came with hippie neighbors that didn't seem to do any yard work. It was not the best house they looked at but it was a short walk to campus and the school of Ed.

She still hadn't recovered from the first time she brought Justin over and he called it a dump. The last owner promised to fix it up and they made a list together. He put a new towel rack in the master bathroom but the rest of the list was ignored.

She turned off the U-Haul and sunk in the seat, she just wanted to fall asleep. The sun was going down but the humidity hung like an invisible fog over the coming night. This was the third trip today, and she had cried each time they left. She watched her sister pull up to park on the street in the rearview mirror. Nikki knew this was better and when the boys got out of the car, she had to have a smile on her face. It broke her heart seeing how sad Justin was to leave the house, but they couldn't stay. It wasn't just the money. The memories were killing her.

Donny had rebuilt every inch of that house. She didn't just lose him in the house, she survived both miscarriages there. When they were both tenured, she expected to grow old together there. She couldn't stay in the house, she never believed in ghosts but his memories haunted her there.

Nikki closed her eyes and squeezed the steering wheel. She prayed for strength; she didn't know where it came from but most days, she found it. She stepped out of the truck. Her sister was arguing with her son as they always did.

"...She's not perfect if she doesn't live in Chicago Hon," Jules put the oversized box in Nate's arms. "So Professor Morgan, where do we start?"

Nikki went past him to her son and pulled him into a hug. She needed it, felt strength from holding him even as he squirmed.

"Mom?" he wanted out of the hug.

"I'm gonna miss the house too, but we gotta make this work, Sweetpea."

Justin nodded and slipped out of the hug. Ray stepped out of the car and looked at them. "I'm sad about the old house too."

Nikki laughed but didn't give the boy a hug. She and Donny had spent more time with Ray then some parents did with their own kids. She loved the boy and the bond he had with her son but as he got older, she felt uncomfortable attention from him. She caught him staring at her from time to time.

"Mom!" Ray suddenly ran across the yard. Bill and Sarah Smith were at the front steps to the house waiting. Ray's mother was holding a casserole pan.

"Surprise!" Nikki said just before her son saw his friends jump out of Ray's parent's car. Robert and Jonah ran across the yard both gave Ray and Justin high fives.

"What are you guys doing here?"

Robert lived back in the old neighborhood, but Jonah lived closer to the new house.

"Sleep-over in the new house!" Nikki smiled.

"No way!" Justin gave an enormous smile to her. Nikki felt a weight being lifted off her shoulders. Jules and Nate ignored it as they opened the back of the truck, all that remained were boxes and she clearly had her son help.

"Once we get the boxes in, we're going to get Noble Romans and you guys can watch Sammy in your room."

"You have a TV in your room?" Robert asked.

"I know!" Ray laughed as they headed towards the boxes.

Nikki walked over to the Smiths while the boys raced to the boxes. Sarah Smith handed the Casserole over to her husband. They melted into a hug.

"How you holdin' up darlin'?" Sarah held her tighter. "You're wasting away."

"I'll go supervise the boys," Bill went into the house. Nikki was out of town at a conference when Donny had his stroke. Sarah beat the ambulance to their house. She had dropped off Ray for their first day back at school after Christmas Break. She had known something was wrong when Justin was late.

"I just wish Justin understood why I had to leave."

Sarah pulled her towards their new house. "They are gonna grow-up fast now you just buckle up, and let's get some food in ya."

CHAPTER THREE

"T-Minus Six minutes until Sammy Terry!" Jonah tapped his watch. It was already late; they helped with boxes as Auntie Jules and Mom were still cleaning pizza plates. They went to the back of the house toward his new room. It was weird not having stairs to run up, his room had always been upstairs. They barely had enough room to fit their sleeping bags on the floor and Justin was happy he had his bed. Smiley already said he was going to sleep downstairs. Once they were in the room laughing and having a good time, he saw Smiley relax.

He finally took his boots off, and everyone gagged at the smell. Jonah twisted the knob on the window and threatened to stick the boots outside. The window screen saved the boots. Smiley threatened to beat his ass but Jonah was a big kid for 8th grade.

"Put em in the hall." Justin laughed. Jonah threw them out like he was dumping a grenade.

Jonah and Smiley got along instantly. They had things in common. Jonah knew punk rock from his older brother and was their smartest friend. He was smarter than many of the teachers they had in elementary school and often made jokes that only the parents laughed at. Justin once heard Jonah's father say "for a genius you don't have any sense." Because as book smart as he was he got them in trouble all the time. If they did something silly nine times out of ten it was Jonah's idea.

Robert was his friend almost as long as Ray, he lived in the neighborhood when they were younger. His parents were professors too but in music school. His dad plays Jazz music and his mother teaches people to sing. Robert told him that is why his parents didn't like being the only black family in the neighborhood. Everyone treated them nicely on the surface, but there was something else going on. Robert told him it was hard to explain. His mother told him once that some people just don't understand how nice Robert and his family are.

"I don't see how you can listen to that punk rock shit," Robert laughed. His house was a musical home, he had been playing piano and guitar since he could walk but he didn't like it. He loved Star Wars and comic books. That is why he and Justin first became friends.

Justin smiled. "It just sounds like noise."

Jonah shook his head. "It is really hard music to play."

"It just sounds like they are banging on shit to me," Ray said as he got his strip of floor positioned to watch Sammy Terry.

"The drums sound crazy I'll give you that," Robert leaned back with an issue of DP 7. It was a comic book in the new Marvel universe.

"That's the last issue I heard they are canceling it," Justin pointed at the comic. "The guy at 25th said the new Marvel Universe was a bust."

"Just an X-men rip off anyways," added Ray.

Now Smiley squirmed, these comic book arguments could last hours and he wanted nothing to do with it. Neither did Jonah, he liked a few comics, but mostly stopped reading them when he got into punk. He reached over to Smiley's backpack that had a couple tapes in it. "You have DK in here?" He found a tape and raised his eyebrows. Jonah went up to the tape player Justin had inherited from his father's workshop basement. His tapes consisted of a Duran Duran album and a bunch of Weird Al tapes. Jonah pushed play and a few seconds chaotic noises filled the room. Jonah turned it down as he started and stopped the tape.

"Hear listen to this," Jonah gave a devilish grin. The speakers seemed to explode with sound. Justin couldn't make sense of it until a screaming voice repeated. "Nazi Punks, Nazi Punks, FUCK OFF!" Justin couldn't believe his ears. His parents, his father most of all swore in front of him. Ray swore all the time even though his mom had told them 'Those words for adults.' He had never heard anything like it in a song so he burst out in laughter.

Ray laughed too; Robert shook his head.

"You never heard a song swear before?" Smiley asked him.

Jonah was already in Smiley's bag again and pulled out a tape that was marked 'Circle Jerks/Minor Threat.' He slapped it in the tape deck. "Wait till you hear 'World up my Ass', my brother has all this stuff."

"That reminds me who is going to introduce me to Emily." Smiley was nodding his head like he had already kissed her. He seemed sure they were destiny.

"Emily McRoberts?" Jonah shook his head. "Her brother is in marching band with my brother. She is super cute but she is moving dude, like far away."

The next song came on and it was equally as loud and fast played and just as quick it was over. It didn't say anything funny but it was fast and loud. "What did he say?"

Jonah turned down the volume. He and Smiley said the lyrics together "I'm innocent until I'm proven guilty! Deny Everything! Deny..."

"Deny what?" Ray looked up from an issue of Hellblazer comic. "Wait that is the whole song?

Smiley laughed, "You dorks would love the Misfits they are into singing about all that horror bullshit you like."

Robert picked up a tape and looked at the fold-out. "Why don't you have a Mohawk like this dude?"

"In Chicago, we have a crew of Skinheads, everybody shaves their heads," Smiley looked at Robert. "We ain't the racist kind we got black friends. I mean there are a couple black skins." Robert didn't know what he was talking about at all. Smiley kept going. "We go to shows they're like concerts but smaller and people slam dance. It looks crazy like people are..."

"We have punk shows in Bloomington my brother goes to them all the time. He said he would take me but my mom doesn't want us slamming."

"...Does Emily go to shows?" Smiley laughed. "I know the dude at the record store told me most of your shows are in basements."

"Dude is that all you think about?" Ray shook his head.

"Hey, Sammy!" Justin yelled as the show switched on. He turned the volume nod on the small TV that had been set up in their kitchen at the old house. Jonah turned off the tape. The Creepy intro music started.

"In the dead of night when the moon is high and ear winds blow and the banshees cry, and the moonlights casts an unearthly glow. Arise my love with tales of unearthly woe."

Smiley laughed as the coffin opened and the green-faced horror host lifted himself from a coffin to introduce *Dracula has Risen from the Grave*. He and Ray were the most devoted to watching Sammy. That is why he slept over so many Fridays, whenever a new episode was on, and that was more often than not. They would cocoon themselves in sleeping bags in the living room to watch whatever movie Sammy offered up. During the school year, they would fall asleep but they would turn on the VCR to tape it. If they fell asleep, they ended up with a morning double feature because Channel 4 showed hilarious Kungfu movies in *Black Belt Theater* after. The mouth never matched the words but the fights were cool and sometimes people flew around.

"That spider is on a frickin' string dude," Smiley laughed. They didn't care It was Sammy and they all loved it. For the first time, Justin wasn't thinking about the movie. His mind wandered and he laughed just thinking that it was so crazy a band named a song World Up my Ass. He knew there must be more and found himself looking at the tapes in his cousin's bag. He had needed the laugh, maybe he should check it all out.

CHAPTER FOUR

"Karate Kid III? Are you Serious?" Justin's jaw was on the floor.

He would rather have seen the new Indiana Jones movie again, or Ghostbusters 2 and both those movies were playing out by the mall at the brand new 11 screen movie theater. It was Smiley's last day in town he picked the corniest movie possible that was playing downtown at the ancient three-screen theater the Von Lee. That theater had been on the border between campus and downtown since 1927.

"Dude, Karate Kid III!" Jonah gave him a weird look. "So many unanswered questions from the first two we have to see it."

Robert shrugged but Ray was just as confused. None of them remembered Jonah being a huge fan of Daniel-son and Mister Miyagi. His Mother grabbed the keys to her car, Aunt Jules had offered to drive them but her hair looked like a road-killed bird and her eyes were barely open. It was almost noon, and all of them had slept in.

"Shotgun!" Jonah yelled.

"There is no shotgun in my mom's car." Justin ran down the steps and was first in the garage. They piled in his mother's ford and took the short drive downtown. They could've walked but the concept of how close they were to downtown Bloomington had not sunk in yet. They had always lived on the outskirts of town. While nothing was more than 10 minutes away to Justin downtown felt really far away. A place he only went to on Tuesday after dad got home to go to the comic book store.

He had spent time in Chicago, visiting his aunt and cousin, but they normally came here to get out of the city. Bloomington is a college town, one hour drive south of Indianapolis. The majority of its population is students. The region had a boom in the early 20th century producing the limestone that built many buildings in New York City. As such the campus takes up a big chunk of the town and the majority of the campus is built out of harsh grey limestone. The town is surrounded by thin woods and hills that don't exist north of Indianapolis. Apparently, the glaciers stopped short of Bloomington back in the day leaving some hills.

When his parents graduated from the University of Chicago Donald and Nikki Morgan had never lived outside of Chicago. They were offered positions at a couple universities but only two offered to hire them both, Florida International in Miami and Indiana. The decision was not a hard one. They missed Chicago but loved life in Bloomington and they became rock stars at the school of Education since teaching teachers was a passion for them.

Justin didn't always understand the commentary his parents made about his hometown. Sometimes they talked about it like it was the best place in the world. Other times they complained that they were surrounded by ignorance; his mom often said she loved Bloomington but hated Indiana. Justin only knew when he visited his grandparents or Aunt in Chicago, he had fun but was ready to get back in a few days. He loved Bloomington, he loved Indiana.

They pulled into the parking lot and they were pointed towards the large blue building across from the western edge of campus. The university considered it an eyesore but the big blue building with a sign written in red futuristic font gave him a smile. Spaceport was supposed to be the best of three arcades in town, but he had never been there. The mall had Aladdin's Castle and that is where they had burned hundreds of gold tokens, on the north side there was a place called the Rack and Cue. It was a pool hall that added video games a few years back, the Rack was smoke-filled and had been off-limits.

Justin thought he understood now. He would've not been into the plan if they told him ahead of time. They were not going to the movie.

"You all have money for the movie?" Mom handed Justin a twenty "Pay for your cousin, okay?"

Justin felt guilt but he thought about how many video game tokens the movie money would give them, they could play a bunch and still have money left for ice cream. They walked slowly as a group toward the front of the theater and Jonah watched Mom's car as it pulled away. Justin walked up to the Karate Kid poster and shook his head at it.

"Were not going to the movie Dumbass," Smiley smacked him on the shoulder. Justin turned to see Jonah crossing the street.

"I know that," Justin said but started to worry about his mom showing up early to pick them up. What if she saw them?

"Yeah, let's go to Spaceport," Ray waited for a car to pass before he and Smiley followed him crossing in the middle of the street. Robert stayed with him and stared at the movie poster and back to Justin. He shrugged.

Justin looked at the Spiderman digital watch his father gave him. They had until 3:15 when his mom or Aunt Jules came back to get them. He looked around almost sure that his mother watched them, he didn't want to cross the street or walk away from the theater. He couldn't believe it but he started to form arguments for seeing the movie.

Robert looked nervous too. They were good kids; they didn't lie to their parents they almost never get in trouble ever unless Jonah thought of something crazy. Smiley and Jonah were almost to the corner door of Spaceport.

"We could just see the movie," Robert said sheepishly "Meet them afterward." Neither of them wanted to. Every time they went to Aladdin's Castle at the mall Jonah told them about Spaceport. He told them about games like Time Pilot and Gyruss two games they didn't have at the mall. Jonah came to Spaceport with his brother all the time. He thought of all the times he felt jealous listening to those stories. Here was his chance. He felt warm under his windbreaker and the guilt wiped away. He didn't want to look like a wuss.

Justin walked towards to curb, he looked down the road towards downtown. The street was filled with cars and the sidewalks were packed with people and suddenly Bloomington didn't feel so small. It was just a few inches but staring at the pavement on Kirkwood Ave felt like a million-mile drop. A car moved slowly past playing rock music as loud as a concert. When it was past Justin took the step and Robert followed. They jogged a bit to catch–up.

When they got closer to the building, they heard music again. It sounded like a car, as they got closer it was like someone was turning a stereo up slowly. It sounded familiar now. Twenty-hours ago it would have sounded like noise but now he knew what it was. Punk rock was playing around the corner. It was a little different from the style they heard the night before the singer sang with harmony. The chorus was had a Woah oh, and his cousin knew the song. He sang along as they turned the corner.

"What band is it?" Justin asked.

They stood by the front door of the arcade and Justin discovered the music was not coming from a car. A boombox covered in duct-tape and band stickers leaned up against a bike rack blasting the area with a sonic assault. A black kid with Bob Marley hair sat cross-legged bobbing his head to the beat and dragging on a cigarette. Another guy leaned up against the rack smoking. His hair was long, he wore a leather jacket covered in patches and had boots that were laced up almost to his knees. He nodded at Jonah.

"You seen my brother?" Jonah asked and turned back to his friends. "This is my brother's friend Lucas."

Lucas took a long drag on his cigarette. He shook his hair back; Justin was surprised to see earrings in both of his ears. "Nah, not since last night."

The song that was playing ended and another started. They were just blasting music as people walked by. A group of students wearing backpacks ignored them as they walked past. Someone across the street at the campus shook her head at them and a woman walked down Kirkwood plugging her ears.

Smiley asked Lucas for a cigarette.

"What are you ten years old? Hell no."

Robert started in the arcade door and Justin decided to follow even though Smiley and Jonah seemed to want to hang around outside. Justin opened the first door and there was a tiny room that consisted of a doormat that smelled like spilled soda with a hint of tobacco, someone had tagged the wall with the word 'airlock' and the staff had failed to erase from the wall. They opened the next door and the sounds of video games filled the air. You could hear Pac-Man eating and the sounds of the ghosts on his tail, the beeps, and music of Centipede, the sit-down Star Wars game played the John Williams score and each game had a player with a small audience waiting for a turn.

A woman in a Guns and Roses shirt, torn jeans, and hair teased to look like the Corona of the sun walked past them. Justin got out his money. He wasn't sure what games he wanted to start. MTV played on TV by the Coke and snack vending machines. There were four booths, a couple sat at one of the tables. The guy's hair was cut into a Mohawk and it was stuck straight in the air like a shark fin.

Smiley walked to the booth and sat down with them. He never came and asked for money. He sat there talking to the punkers. That was fine, more games for Justin.

Justin spent five dollars failing to make it past three levels of Gyruss. The game was similar to Galaga, that was one he had mastered through several levels at the mall. Instead of just going side to side shooting up Gyruss spun around and you hand to shoot at ships that spun at you. After each round, you would warp to another planet, and they moved faster and faster. He liked the game but sucked at it. He waited for Galaga to open up when Smiley came around the corner.

"Come on we're going to the park."

Justin turned to see the guy with the Mohawk leaving, and it was like Smiley was being pulled by his gravity. Robert walked up to them; they were all out of money. Justin had planned to save the rest for Jiffy Treat ice cream. Jonah and Ray walked up to them.

"Come on everyone is hanging at the park," Smiley backed towards the door.

"What park?" Ray asked.

"People's Park," Jonah pointed at the door with his thumb.

Ray, Robert, and Justin all shared a look. The park was on the same block as the movie theater, just around the corner. Only a bike shop separated the theater from the park. It was the size of a small parking lot, a little green space in the middle of the half-mile long business strip that connected the campus with the town courthouse square. Besides the library, it was the only spot that didn't have a store on it. They were on the way to the comic bookstore once and his father called Weirdo Park.

Smiley and Jonah were already out the door. Ray shrugged and followed. Again, Robert and Justin were last out. The boom box was gone, it may have been a coincidence but a campus police car was now parked on the street a few doors down at the White Rabbit gift shop. When they turned the corner, they saw Smiley and Jonah moving with the pack of punk rockers. They jay-walked across the street just after a large truck drove past, Lucas was at the lead them using his boom box like a Pied Piper.

Justin, Ray, and Robert used the cross-walk; they walked slowly in front of the theater and the bike shop. There was a knee-high wall that separated the sidewalk from the park. There were benches at the back of the park; they were filled with older looking hippie types and who were drinking from bottles still in bags. The punks sat on the front wall, their legs dangling into the park, but a few sat cross-legged making them look like birds perched on powerlines.

Lucas set up the boom box in the grass as he searched through his friend's bag for a tape. Smiley and Jonah were comfortable taking space on the wall. Justin looked at his Spiderman watch, the time was 2:55. His mom would be there soon, he quickly unhooked the watch and put in his pocket hoping no one saw it. He didn't know if anyone caught his embarrassment. Justin took a seat on the wall.

Someone had given Smiley a smoke, he was acting like he knew how to hold it but he could barely breathe it in.

"You ain't no smoker," said the guy with a mohawk. Several of the older punks, some of whom looked old enough to be in college laughed.

Smiley eyed up the crowd and puffed his chest, "fuck you, man, I'm from Chicago, not some pussy-ass little town."

Justin cringed at the fighting words, but the Mohawker just laughed and dragged on his smoke. A conversation happened, but Justin couldn't follow it. Smiley kept talking about Chicago he must have thought that it made him look cool because he said In Chicago thirty times.

Lucas rolled his eyes. "Chi-town. Real cool."

There was more, Justin tuned it out and just kept looking around. The real entertainment was watching at the characters at the front of the park, there was a woman with her head almost shaved except her bangs, a second guy with a Mohawk this one shorter, and a circle of smokers by the boom box including a guy in all black with an Umbrella in the sun. The older weirdos sat in the back of the park. There was hippie tuning a guitar, a guy doing Tai-chi, a woman with a large hiking backpack setting up a tent and a loud black man wearing a Vietnam Vet baseball hat who was telling a story about the war that could be heard across the park clearly. A guy wearing spiked collars on his wrists handed him a blue quarter piece of paper with band names on it.

"Show Friday night at the Savage House, Three bands three bucks."

No one in this park cared that they looked weird, or that normal people were staring. They didn't care that someone might judge them. He thought of all the times he was bullied at school for liking Star Trek or carrying a Science Fiction book his father gave him. School had been torture at times, and he just wanted people to leave him alone.

Justin watched Lucas walk up to the Vet and sit down. Jonah leaned over and whispered to him.

"That's Zoe the Vet, my brother says he can't work cuz' he is crazy as a shithouse rat. They call the back of the park Skid Row, Zoe buys punks beer for extra money."

That was interesting but Justin knew the time had passed he was nervous about getting to the theater parking lot. His nervous energy got his heart beating fast. The boom box suddenly played the song he knew. Nazi Punks Fuck Off. He felt the energy of the song, the fast beat, the angry shouting. There was anger he had felt for months that he didn't know how to express. He had cried so much over his father, but he felt something else. He was supposed to have a dad. He loved his dad, he didn't just feel sad, he felt angry, and that music may have been about Nazis but the anger just felt good. The attitude just felt good.

This was better than the movie.

Ray still had on a watch. "Hey, we gotta go." Jonah pointed to the back of the park; they normally left that theater by the emergency exit in the back. He pointed to the back of the park past Skid Row. There was a massive hole in the center of the park that they had to walk around. There was a sign that had drawings of a sculpture that was going to be put in the park. As they walk past Justin looked in the hole that was the size of home plate.

It was probably in his mind but the hole seemed unusually deep he didn't even see a bottom. Ray must have had the same thought because he spit a loogie into the hole. Justin listened long after his friends walked past. The spit and snot combo that was a product of mild allergies Ray always dealt with in the summer was big enough to land with a splat. It never came, Justin didn't have time to dwell on it as he ran to catch up to his friends.

Smiley walked at the front of their group with his smoke hanging off his big lip. He seemed to not remember that he was a little kid and acted like a tough guy three times his size. It looked silly to Justin he couldn't imagine how it looked to these older folks. When they passed the older group Lucas was still talking to Zoe.

Zoe wore a Vietnam War Vet baseball that had pins on it for battled he survived. He leaned back holding a large bottle in a paper bag. He was a dark-skinned black man with a short fro popping out from under his hat. His eyes were bloodshot.

He was animated as he talked on. "Shit, when I got back, I had leave and could've come back here but I spent my cash on a chevy and road-tripped down to the Mexican Rockies. Finest weed you ever up in those hills, boy let me tell..."

Lucas laughed. "Zoe there ain't no Mexican Rockies."

"Motherfucker you been there? Cuz' I was there. Happy as fuck to be alive."

"There are Canadian Rockies and the Rocky Mountains but there ain't no fucking Mexican Rockies."

Jonah laughed. Zoe turned to look at him. "Look at these young bloods," Zoe took a swing off of the drink in his bottle.

Smiley stopped to posture but Jonah for once showed some sense and pushed him forward. Lucas laughed and that was enough to make Smiley angrier. He was ready to yell at them, probably something about Chicago. Further down the bench, an older man sat by himself. It was unfortunate that he was there. He was balding with unkempt hair in a U around the base of his skull. He was wearing an unseasonably thick winter coat zipped halfway and under it, he had on a pajama onesie, that was unzipped enough to show off some chest hair. He had on headphones that were blasting static, loud enough that they could hear it five feet away. He was writing in an upside-down notebook reading aloud as he did so.

"...We can add water to a red barren planet too hot to support life and cool it. I will supply you with a life making kit..." He looked up for just a moment but his eyes connected with Smiley.

"Fuck you looking at freak?" Smiley yelled at the man and kicked the bench next to him. The crazy man didn't react just kept writing in his notebook faster.

"...and a traveling rope to get there..."

Jonah towered over the crazy man and it looked at the notebook. "Holy shit, you guys gotta see the crazy shit he is writing."

Lucas jumped up off the bench. "Hey back off you little shits, leave Fred alone."

Jonah pointed at the guy and laughed. "Wait this guy is Electric Fred?"

"More like shithouse crazy Fred," Smiley laughed too. Fred finally lifted up his pen but still, his eyes were on his notebook. He shook his head and spoke softly as if whispering to the notebook. "Be careful they don't want to see it."

"You guys hang out with this fuckin' freak?"

"Get the fuck out of here!" A woman's voice came from the parking lot. Justin turned to see a woman standing there. Justin's jaw almost dropped. She was beautiful but in a way he had never seen in his life. Dyed black hair, a slightly ripped shirt that read Sisters of Mercy, she had a ring in her nose and tattoos like a sailor on her arm. Behind all the darkness in her style were sharp blue eyes that were prettiest he had ever seen. All the boys in the group were stunned by the sight of her, well except Smiley.

"What are you his goth bodyguards?"

"What are you Fisher-Price's first Skinhead?"

"I got it, Lisa," Lucas grinned as if to totally laugh us off that any of this was any kind of threat.

"We didn't mean nothing," Justin pulled on Smiley who tried to plant his feet as if he was going to fight. He didn't resist as Justin helped push him into the alley behind the park. His cousin wanted to look like he was standing his ground. Justin looked back Lucas stood with his arms out ready to fight. Zoe stood up looking massive behind him.

"Fred don't hurt nobody," Zoe spoke in a comically deep voice.

Fred suddenly jumped forward and grabbed Ray. "I feel your anger," With his free hand, he pointed to the center of the park. "Oh, sure this space was or is for the community now but it is anger and hate that opens us up now."

Justin jumped forward and pulled on Ray's arm. Lisa grabbed Fred's free arm and tried to pull him the other way. Jonah grabbed Justin and for a moment they were a chain. Fred closed his eyes and screamed. It shook Justin he didn't let go. He heard a crack like thunder but the skies were blue. He closed his eyes and when he opened them Fred was back on the bench.

Lisa sat down next to Fred. It looked like she wanted to comfort him but it was clear she was nervous to touch him. "Come on Fred let's just go to the Spoon I am starting my shift."

Justin felt guilty about laughing at this man who was clearly crazy. Fred turned back and looked at them as he walked away with Lisa. Their eyes locked for a moment. Justin thought he heard his voice but his lips didn't move.

See, all of you see it.

"He's fucking crazy as hell," Smiley barked.

Lucas stepped closer and spoke just above a whisper. "Fred is harmless, if you yell at him again this whole park will beat your little asses."

"It's cool, cool, we're cool Lucas," Jonah said his face had turned beet red.

Justin almost jumped out of his skin when they turned the corner to the parking lot and saw his mother's car. She was reading a book. Ray opened the back door first.

"How was the movie?"

"It sucked," Smiley said as he got in the car last. Justin looked at his mother who had a knowing smile on her face. She knew they didn't go to the movie, but something told him that she didn't care. She put the car in drive.

"Yeah, I am sure you will tell me all about it."

CHAPTER FIVE

Smiley pushed open his door without knocking. "What are you doing fuck face?"

This had been the first ten minutes Justin had alone in his new room since the move. He was unpacking his books. He had a shelf set aside for the Science Fiction books that had been his father's. From Asimov to Zelazny his father had left him a collection that now would be shelved in his room. He had been thinking about the Dune books. He had read those with his father and they had just finished the third book with his dad sitting by his bed at night. They didn't do it every night but the idea that he would have to read them alone felt daunting. His father always explained the parts he didn't understand.

"Putting away books," Justin was tired of his cousin and was glad that he and Auntie Jules were going back home. Smiley still had his boots on but he dropped on Justin's blue bean bag. "I used your mom's double tape deck and made this." He held up a cassette tape. "Minor Threat, Circle Jerks, DK and Suicidal Tendencies as much as I could fit into ninety-minutes."

He had written all the song titles in his crappy hand-writing on the paper card that wrapped around the cassette. The truth was he planned on asking Jonah to make him a tape as he knew he had access to all his brother's records. He gave his cousin a smile.

"The park was kinda dorky, but you should hang out there," Smiley shrugged. "I mean it's the best you got."

Justin rolled his eyes. He knew where Smiley and his friends hung out, he had heard the stories a dozen times this week. "You hang out in a Dunkin' Donuts parking lot..."

"Sometimes but we go to the drinking alley and..."

Justin threw the tape on his bed and went back to his books. Smiley stopped so he must have figured out that he didn't care about Chicago stories. Justin held a copy of his father's favorite book Martian Time-Slip close to his face. He knew it was in his mind but his books smelled like his Dad's office at the old house. Smiley watched him smell the book. Justin didn't care what he thought about it.

"Sorry about Uncle Donny," Smiley had said it before but he didn't know else what to say. "At least you had a dad right, my dad just..."

Justin felt guilty. He never in their life thought what it must have been like for his cousin. They were both too young to remember when his father left. Justin nodded he didn't know what to say.

"Yeah, so Jonah is cool man you guys should come up to Chicago this summer. We can go see Naked Raygun, I put a few songs on the B side." Smiley backed out of the room. In the morning he and Auntie Jules would head back to Chicago. Justin and his mother would be alone in their new house for the first time. He pushed the door shut and turned to look at the boxes still unpacked in his new room. He looked up at the small TV and considered turning it on, it was funny because he always wanted a TV in his room but now at this moment, he didn't give a shit. His eyes caught the tape.

He walked over to his stereo; his dad's old record player also had a tape deck. He snapped the tape in, took a deep breath and hit play.

Lisa stepped out of the kitchen holding the plate with the untoasted cheese sandwich for her most regular customer. She couldn't convince Fred Curtis to leave the park with her but he was like clockwork showing up at his normal time. He ordered a cheese sandwich and a Coke. He didn't go to the counter and order he just came to get it when she put it on the counter. She added it to his tab that he paid off the second day of every month.

"Thank you, Cindi," Fred spoke and smiled at her, she long ago gave up correcting him with her actual name. He had given her many names since she worked at the spoon only correctly naming her twice. The other baristas didn't get even a name or eye-contact from Electric Fred unless it was the day he got his disability payment, and then he would ask them for his bill.

The local punks she saw at shows also got her name wrong too, calling her Scary Leeza, a name she got for dressing in vampire queen outfits for shows. In Bloomington that meant more dingy basements than concert halls. A few came into the spoon but it was hard to miss her walking around campus as she was the most goth person in the small town.

None of that seemed to bother Fred, it was six months before he even took his headphones off when he came to the counter. The rumors were true. It was a radio he listened to and it was tuned to static most of the time. Although from time to time she saw him almost dancing in his seat as he wrote in his notebooks. Always writing or drawing in his notebooks.

She had worked at the Spoon since mid-second semester the year before. It was the oldest running coffee shop in Bloomington. One block north of Kirkwood and the business strip is connected by an alley to all the activity of downtown. It was in an old red house that had been turned into a coffee joint in the seventies. It was the only place that offered her a job despite lots of restaurant experience. Lisa was unwilling to compromise who she was, goth and proud of it. The customers who were mostly IU professors didn't care or even seem to notice. Some of them were parked there long enough to basically offer office hours. She had seen several students show up to talk about classes. They played endless Jazz during the day and played The Cure and Depeche Mode after the owner Jeff went home.

Lisa loved the Spoon. The shop was a short walk from her dorm and that was important after she closed the place, she was walking home close to midnight three nights a week. Her regulars didn't care that she was a weirdo. Didn't care that a clearly mentally ill man in Fred hung out there beside them, that attitude was part of what made the spoon a special place.

"Hey Fred what are you writing?" She always tried to engage him.

He froze in step with his cheese sandwich and turned around looking like Doc Brown from Back to the Future. He shushed her and kept walking back to his table. Lisa came around the counter with the purpose of cleaning a table that had been left for her despite the bus tub positioned clearly by the door.

Fred drew in his notebook with a ballpoint pen. He had the notebook upside down and was drawing a picture with his left hand. Lisa couldn't help looking, she had a long interest in Fred's notebooks, they were all forty sheets wide ruled. The color of the cover didn't matter, but he started a notebook almost every morning. During most days he filled an entire notebook.

Today he was sketching, the drawing more elaborate than most of the ones he drew. He had sketched the park around the corner that they had been in a few hours earlier. It was rough but she recognized the basic layout of the park she walked past daily.

"Wow Fred that is a great drawing," She didn't know the park very well having never spent time there. She knew if she grew up here in Bloomington, that park would have been a second home. They didn't have much of a hang-out forty-five-minute drive north in Southport the Indianapolis suburb where she grew up. The weirdos just had a Dairy Queen parking lot. It was near a record store and one of their friends was a blizzard jockey hiding his Mohawk under his DQ hat.

Fred pulled his headphones off and they kept blasting static that she could faintly hear. "I have informed the Prime Minister."

Lisa looked around to see if anyone was listening to them. She wanted him to explain but didn't want Fred to get mocked by anyone sitting nearby. He trusted her enough over time to be honest with her. He knew she didn't mock him. She knew that Fred was ill, but was fascinated to know more about him. He was not sleazy like some of the professors who were regulars and hit on the women working there. He was not sane, but Lisa could tell that Fred was a genius, an intelligent man tortured by his own mind.

"The Prime-Minister of what Fred?"

His pen stopped while he thought about it, his eyes never left the paper he was drawing.

"I'm not a spy, you understand. I report to whatever agency is best equipped for the situation. The Chinese are the best hope we have."

"I don't think China has a Prime-Minister Fred," Lisa whispered.

He shook a finger at her. He reached back into his backpack and pulled out a notebook that she assumed was yesterday's work. He flipped through the papers every inch was densely packed with words and drawings most abstract but a few were faces. He found the page he needed. He pointed at writing that looked different from his. He flipped a page and the sheet was filled with letters she recognized from fortune cookies. Chinese conge.

"Eh, I didn't do that."

"How do you share those with the Prime Minister?"

He looked around. He whispered so low she almost didn't hear him. "I have a drop-box."

Lisa felt so bad for Fred. He was a nice enough fellow, who sometimes had fits of rage that he mostly kept outside. Only once did she hear him yelling in the Spoon bathroom. His clothes didn't fit, his onesie that he wore under his unseasonal jacket smelled a little gamey. Today it was the prime minister of China, last week he was planning trips to Mars by tether rope.

"So, what do you need China's help with?"

He put up a finger for a moment before he kept drawing. He worked for several minutes drawing a gaping hole at the center of the park. He filled in the center with a thick block of black ink. Then he drew what looked like ghosts rising from it. He only paused to take bites of his sandwich Lisa couldn't stop watching him draw.

"Are those ghosts?"

Fred stopped and looked at her as if she had said something offensive. "Ah, if only something so simple," He took the last bite of his sandwich and closed his notebook. "You don't want them seeing you, Cindi. You don't have to believe in them, they believe in you."

Like that he was gone, only stopping to put his plate in the bus tub.

CHAPTER SIX

Justin pushed the button for the garage door and grabbed his bike. Auntie Jules already had her car packed. Smiley was talking to Jonah who stood with his skateboard that he had built his with parts from the skate shop with his brother. Justin had to move boxes to get his embarrassing generic skateboard that his mother had bought at Kmart. The wheels were huge but he could barely do an ollie. He felt uneasy walking out to meet Jonah who immediately pointed at it.

"Nice monster truck wheels." Smiley laughed at his cousin but gave him a hug.

Mom and Auntie Jules looked like they were going to cry when they hugged. They did this every time one of the families left town.

"Play Jonah the tape," Smiley said as he got in the car.

Mom came around the car and put her arm around him. They waved as the car headed down the road. There was a quiet moment the only sound Jonah popping ollies on his skate in the driveway.

"I have to go into the office; Sweetpea, what are you doing today?"

Justin shrugged. He was about to say watch movies.

"Skate!" Jonah said as the board squirted out from under him landing in the yard.

"Don't go far," Mom said. It was the worst thing she could have said because Jonah the king of bad ideas started to think of how far they could go. They waited until Mom had packed her backpack and started the walk to campus. Justin counted his money he managed to save five dollars.

"Spaceport isn't far," Jonah said as they pushed their skates down roads with less traffic "I mean she said not to go far, I mean Indianapolis is far." The arcade was not far, technically Jonah was correct but that is not where Justin wanted to go if he was being honest.

"Okay, but first we're going to 25th."

25th Century Five and Dime was at the bottom of a stone staircase in the basement of a building that housed one of the city's most famous restaurants. The Uptown Café served pretty much the same menu as Denny's but it was considered fancy. Going down the stairs was in many ways like walking into another world.

The sign was easy to miss but it was subtitled Comics, games and more. Operated by Greg Thompson, his family also owned the Book Corner, and the Book Nook near campus. The store had to be a major health hazard for Thompson who was always there. If he had a Dentist appointment, there would be a sign on the door, as there was no one to fill in for him. The door had a wooden frame the glass taped up with posters, it stuck every time you pushed it open. It also took a second effort to get it open.

"Hey," Justin said as he walked in. Thompson didn't look up from the issue of Thor he was reading. He never did. This space should never have housed a store. It was musty, hardly any air or light made it in the basement. The ceiling was nothing but exposed pipes, random workshop lights hung from the ceiling. Every spot was filled with plastic-wrapped back issues. Marvel upfront, DC in the back, random titles in the middle and games in alphabetical order.

The new comics came on Tuesday so there was nothing new he or Jonah needed. Used comics came in all the time so they both started looking. In the last year, Justin had faded away from superhero comics and was starting to get into horror comics. Ray had said it was a side effect of all the Sammy Terry they watched. They all loved Hellblazer which had an adult content warning on it but Thompson didn't give a shit.

He looked through the Warren comics, he was had collected every copy of the 70's horror comics Eerie and Creepy he could get his hands on. Thompson and his dad always talked about Science Fiction when his father would bring him here. They talked about Philip K Dick who they both loved and a writer named John Brunner who Thompson kept telling him to read.

Jonah flipped through comics down the line. "You wanna hang at the park after this?"

Justin did, part of him was nervous but he didn't want to show it.

"Ray hated the park," Jonah laughed.

It was true, Ray didn't like the music, didn't feel comfortable around the weirdos.

"You know he is going to be a jock just like his buddies on the basketball team." Jonah was already tall considering they were all still entering 8th grade. He was recruited for the basketball team but he hated sports. Ray, Justin, and Robert all liked to play Basketball. Ray who played on their garage door hoop with his father was going to play in high school. He knew as much about hoop as he did horror movies.

"So?" Justin thought he knew what he meant.

"Just saying the jocks and rednecks at school hate my brother, and if we start listening to punk, they are going to hate us too."

"That's stupid why?" He pulled out the third issue of Creepy he didn't have this one with a color drawing of an executioner in a black chopping off a man's head in full detail.

"Cuz looking different scares them."

"Why?"

"I don't know dude they just hate it. Did you like the tape Smiley made you?"

Justin loved it. Listened to it three times in the day he has had it. "Well, I don't need to have a Mohawk to listen to punk."

Justin held up the Creepy comics he could afford. They walked to the counter. Thompson was typing on his register when Justin looked behind his shoulder. There was a hand-drawn poster that read *"If you don't like this universe, you should see the others."* Under the quote the name Philip K Dick.

Justin wondered if that poster was what got his father talking to Thompson who never even thanked him. He silently handed him his change. Jonah was already up the stairs. For a brief moment, Justin caught his reflection on the glass pane of the door. In the odd light, he almost didn't see it, but something was in the reflection standing behind him like the hooded figure on the cover of his comic.

Justin turned and just saw the empty comic shop. He heard the sound of Jonah's skate hitting the sidewalk above on the street. He ran to catch up.

Ray sat in his room reading a comic book. It wasn't the best issue of *Captain America* he was fighting to keep his eyes open and the sound of his brother playing basketball distracted him. Their dad had built the court just under his window. At the time he was excited, they came a long way from the milk crate tied to a tree in the back yard. His wall shook with every bank shot, and his brother was a bad shooter so the sounds he heard all day long were, thunk, thunk and the unending clank of the ball off the back of the rim.

He dropped the comic and sat looking up at the ceiling. He didn't notice when the sounds of the ball had stopped. He was still tired from staying up all night at Justin's new house on Friday. Even though it was Sunday he didn't feel caught up.

He heard the rumble of his brother coming up the stairs. Ray jumped up when the door kicked in and his brother stood there sweating in a Bloomington South Basketball jersey. He bought the shirt, didn't earn it, could even make the freshman team. Ray thought about busting his balls about that fact, but let it go. There had been a time when they were best friends. All Joe cared about was sports, all he thought about was sports. The worst part was he was terrible at them. He had no idea, he thought he was good.

Ray, on the other hand, was a natural, even though it was not his first love he could hoop. He did well at football because he naturally remembered routes, so he dominated at pop-Warner. There was a little resentment between them but it was all one way. Joe hated his younger brother's natural talent and the fact that he didn't even seem to care. He hated the comic books, and the horror movies but kept silent about it.

His brother stood there in the doorway and didn't have to ask. Ray shook his head.

"Come on, let's go hoop."

"Nah, I'm tired." Ray leaned back on the bed and opened his comic book. Joe kicked the bed. Ray looked up in shock. His brother was only one year ahead of him, not much bigger but they had not fought in years. Not since the first time, Joe really hurt him. Their mother put the fear of God into them.

"What the fuck?" Ray stood up. Something stopped him. His brother looked different, his eyes vacant. Ray regretted getting this close. He couldn't step back the bed was right behind him.

"Come on, put down those f***** books and hoop."

Ray didn't know what to say. A part of him wanted to get angry. The tough guy responses all flashed through his mind but he didn't say anything. He was confused they were alone so he didn't worry about what anyone had to say, or his image. He just stood there looking into his brother's eyes. This wasn't like him. Faintly he thought he heard the sounds of the basketball. It must have been his father they were the only three that ever used the court. Ray thought about yelling to his father to come up here and deal with Joe. He heard the ball. Thunk, thunk and the clank of missed shot.

"What's wrong with you?" Ray asked. "Dad!" he yelled loud enough to be heard outside.

"Yeah, call for help you fucking pussy!" Joe's eyes narrowed as their father appeared at the top of the steps almost instantly. Ray breathed a sigh of relief.

"Dad, Joe is acting crazy. Tell him to get out of my room."

Ray counted on his dad. He was always fair and just with them. He was a sweet and compassionate guy. He grew up with a hard military Dad and never wanted to be like their grandpa. Ray waited for his father to tell Joe to leave, but the wait was long. Then he heard the basketball again, on the court outside. Thunk, thunk, and Clank.

"Why don't you go hoop with your brother?"

His father's voice sounded dull, empty. It didn't make sense. Ray turned away from them to look out the window. The wall shook as a ball must've hit the backboard. Ray looked over his brother's shoulder. His father was gone. Joe backed away and waved at him to follow before he walked down the stairs. He was still loudly stepping down the stairs. The sound of the ball on the court kept going. He heard his brother walking down the steps.

Ray ran to the window and his jaw dropped. There was Joe lifting up to take a shot. Ray ran to the stairs and they were empty. He blinked twice, he heard the sounds of a Cincinnati Reds baseball game on the TV. Ray ran down the stairs and found his father half asleep in his chair.

"Dad?"

Bill Smith was startled awake and jumped up in his chair to see his son. Ray must have looked freaked up because his Dad came fully to attention.

"What's wrong son?"

"Were you just upstairs?"

His dad shook his head. "I must've dozed off a little." His father slept through more baseball than he watched but never admitted to it for some reason.

"You were just upstairs; Joe was just upstairs."

His father looked confused at him. He pointed at the TV. "I'm watching the Reds beat the…"

Ray sighed; he didn't even know who they were playing. "The Cubs."

Dad shook his head still drowsy. "Yep, yeah, The Cubbies and your brother is outside throwing up bricks."

Ray didn't understand. He turned and looked out the window, his brother was wearing a blank blue T-shirt. The armpits soaked from the sweat he generated in the summer humidity. Dad pulled the lever on his chair and it snapped back into place.

"You OK son?" He didn't seem to have the energy to stand.

He just ran back up the stairs. He couldn't make sense of any of it. He ran straight to the bathroom. He wanted to splash cold water on his face, he didn't shut the door. He splashed his face and then looked in the mirror. He didn't feel crazy.

He looked back to the stairs and saw his father walking slowly up the stairs. It didn't make any sense he was just here. Ray turned to see his father in the doorway. He was a man that generally carried a smile and a happy tone. Not now at this moment. The confusion was also gone. He stood there silently.

"Why did you take his side?"

His father stood in the doorway. "You'll never be a grown-man reading those kids' books."

Ray's jaw dropped. His father never complained about the comic books before. He even asked him what happened in Captain America whenever he brought a new issue home. Ray felt anger and sadness but after what his father said the last thing, all he wanted to do was cry. He wanted to just escape.

"Can I go to Justin's house?" It was a tall ask on a Sunday. He would need a ride into town. Still, he had stayed there on school nights. His father was oddly still.

"Will Robert be there?" His father asked.

Ray thought nothing of it. He was one of his oldest friends. Had slept over at Robert's house, and he had stayed here. Ray shrugged.

"OK as long as you stay away from the n*****," Bill Smith said coldly as he left the bathroom. That was the one word they were not allowed to say. They could swear at him but his parents joked about not swearing in front of teachers or other parents. The N-word was just not said. The word was like a bomb, Ray didn't know how to react.

Ray stepped slowly into the hallway. His smiley-faced father suddenly looking back to normal started down the stairs. "I'll grab my keys."

CHAPTER SEVEN

Justin bought plastic bags and cardstock for each of the new comics. Putting them safely away was a part of the routine when he stepped back into the sunlight after a trip to Twenty-fifth. Jonah just shoved his into Justin's backpack and thought he was weird for bagging them before even reading them. They grabbed their skateboards and walked up to the street. Justin set his deck down on the sidewalk and sat on it to carefully put away his comics.

"We can go to Spaceport but I only have seventy-five cents left and..."

"Hey Emily," Jonah cut him off.

It was pretty nerdy feeling, Justin felt caught holding his comic books he almost didn't look up to see Emily McRoberts from his old neighborhood standing over him. He stared at her feet. She was wearing two-tone vans, one white sock and a black one.

"What you reading?"

"Uh just stuff," Justin quickly shoved the comic books in his backpack. He finally looked up at her. They were in the shade of the building, but Emily's long blonde hair got blow around in the wind. For the first time, he noticed purple-dyed highlights. They must've been new, or maybe he just looked away so quickly he hadn't noticed before.

"Some dorky shit," Jonah said as if he didn't have comics in the backpack.

"I like comics a little." Emily smiled she was looking down at Justin. "For real, what'cha reading?"

"Uh, it's a Hellblazer spin-off from Swamp Thing, and some horror comics."

She nodded. Justin stood up and kicked his deck into his hands. There was an awkward moment where they stood there in silence.

"Sorry you moved out of the neighborhood, but it is cool you can skate downtown."

"I've always lived here, by downtown I mean." Jonah nervously tapped his thumb on his deck.

Emily smiled at him, she backed away slightly. "I was just heading to Karma."

"Records?" Jonah pointed his thumb east down Kirkwood. The record store was at the far end of the strip closer to the park around the corner from the arcade. "We were just heading there."

"Yeah, the record store. We're going to look for some..." Justin suddenly forgot the names of all the punk bands he had heard over the weekend.

"*Dead Kennedys,*" Jonah pointed at Justin.

"Yeah, Circle uh Jerks," The only other one that came to Justin.

"Wanna walk with me?" Emily must've known the answer because she started walking.

Jonah did most of the talking. They were talking about their favorite songs by *the Dead Kennedys*. Emily liked a band called *Minor Threat* the most. She was going to Karma to get a new record of the singer of that band's new stuff. Justin felt pretty out of it, no idea what they were talking about. He just felt weird walking so close to her. Emily was a girl he saw in fleeting moments. Now they were walking so close that he felt her arm brush up against him twice.

Downtown Bloomington was busy, it was a warm summer day and the humidity hung thick in the air. The five blocks of businesses on Kirkwood Ave that separated the town square from the massive university campus had more traffic when IU was in session, but people were out walking. They cut through a group of college students but the conversation kept going.

"You want to hang at the park after Karma?"

It was like Justin woke from sleep. He knew it was Emily's voice. It took him a minute to process what she was asking them. He nodded as they waited to cross the street. On the next block was a bank and not much further on the opposite side was the public library. Justin felt a lump of something caught in his throat thinking of his dad. They used to go to the library together all the time. It was crazy to think about him now. He couldn't be sad every minute of the day but his father's ghost loomed over him.

They walked past the bank and suddenly there was a parking lot on their right. Jonah seemed to freeze up for a second. Justin and Emily kept walking. The parking lot had a cloud of smoke over it. Several large cars and a few trucks jacked up on large wheels were parked there. The lot was near the bank but it was a public lot. Several people sat in the back of two trucks with the back gate down, every one of them held a cigarette. A couple of them held drinks wrapped in paper bags.

There must've been twenty of them. The women had teased hair that looked like a lion's mane. Most of the guys had short bangs and a tuff of slightly longer hair in the back. The shirts ranged from *Hank Williams Jr.* to *Guns and Roses*. More than one of the vehicles had a front confederate flag license plate and most of the trucks had a gun rack.

"Keep walking," Jonah said just above a whisper. The conversation between them stopped as they felt all the eyes in the parking lot staring at them. It was science Justin realized for every action there is an equal opposite reaction. In this case, it was redneck land three blocks away from People's Park.

Def Leopard's Foolin' jammed out of the speaker's that appeared to be built into the grill of a Blue Chevy Nova parked right against the three-foot concrete wall that separated the sidewalk from the lot. Two large mustached dudes sat on the wall in front of the car.

The one in Hank Jr. shirt took a drag on his smoke. "Skate or die dude." His friends laughed. Someone back in one the trucks called them "freaks." Justin hoped Jonah kept his mouth shut. That would've been the smart thing to do. The problem is Jonah never did the smart thing.

"That your car?" Jonah pointed at the big blue muscle car. "With the speakers in the grill?"

The driver's side door opened and a large man with an ill-fitting *Thin Lizzy* shirt stepped out. He stood up straight. "It's mine."

"You got a rad car dude."

"No, it's not, it's blue."

Justin couldn't help it. He laughed. So did Emily. Hank Jr. shirt dude stepped off the wall and puffed his chest.

"Something funny freak?"

Jonah nodded yes. Emily pulled on his arm to keep him moving. Justin picked up his speed to catch up to them not looking back despite the laughter, and mockery from redneck land. The parking lot creeps all stood and watched them walk away. No one on either side said anything. Emily and Jonah kept their eyes forward. They were halfway down the block when Justin peeked. He had to double-take. The rednecks were already in their spots like nothing happened. They laughed and talked like nothing had happened. The song had changed. He didn't know this one.

"Forget about those fucking assholes," Jonah said.

Justin picked up his pace to stay with the group.

"I'm glad I don't have to go to high school with them," Emily smirked.

Justin cringed inside. He was so happy to hang out with her he had forgotten. She was moving away. He couldn't worry about that now because her point was valid. Most of the parking lot rednecks were Juniors and Seniors who already drove to and from school. A few had probably graduated but were refusing to grow up. Jonah should've thought about that. In just a few months they would see them at school every single day.

Justin didn't fully understand what motivated them. Why they were so offended by the way they looked or the skateboards. Why did they just hang out in the parking lot. "Do they just sit there all day? In a parking lot?"

"No, just till the sun goes down." Jonah pointed at Kirkwood Ave. "Then they drive up and down the street for a couple hours."

"To what waste gas?" Asked Emily.

"They're cruisers, they show off their stupid trucks." Jonah shook his head.

Justin nodded. It wasn't long before they passed People's Park. It was across the street but the regulars were there. The freaks and weirdos were in their spots, talking hanging out as they had the day before. Most were the same exact spot as the day before. Just seeing them made Justin feel better, at least he would not be alone at school. At least a few of the park kids were still in summer school.

They walked around the corner before long they were at the record store. Justin had seen this store when he rode past in the car with Mom and Dad. He had never been to any of the downtown record stores, just Musicland and Disc Jockey at the mall. It was a little thing but as he followed Emily in the door, he got excited.

They passed through a turnstile as they walked in. Every inch of the large room was T-shirts, records, tapes, and CDs. The music playing was super loud and fast. Jonah told him it was Black Flag, a band he had heard mentioned but it was the first time he heard them. All the cassettes and CDs were in long plastic cases and along the walls. The records were in the middle.

Jonah nodded at the guy behind the counter, he had a shaved head and large earrings.

"Hey Emily and Justin this is Whittaker, he plays bass in a couple of bands."

He stood behind the counter as he priced records. "Let me know if I can help you find anything?"

Justin walked to the used cassettes and saw a shelf that was labeled punk/Noise/ Hardcore. He scanned the tapes and the band names made him laugh. *Belgian Waffles, The Hard-ons, The Dickies.* There were a couple names that were not that funny. Justin turned back to see Jonah talking to Emily. She was flipping through CD's and he stood there talking to her just chatting. No other reason but to flirt with her.

He wished he could do that but he was still intimidated to talk to her. She looked up at him and he felt caught. She smiled. "Hey, Justin come here."

Justin walked slowly through the aisles and held his skateboard at his side. "Yeah?"

She held up a red CD "I found it, Fugazi, it has two records on CD they are just called thirteen songs."

"Pretty great record," Whittaker chimed in. "Ian MacKaye did a band in between Embrace and Fugazi called *Egghunt*, just one two-song record we have one copy left in the 7-inches."

"Cool," Emily said as she walked over to the records to look for it.

Jonah watched her walking and shook his head. "Dude she is killing me. She doesn't give a shit about me at all."

Justin just shrugged.

"She clearly likes this dude," Whittaker pointed at Justin.

"Me?" Justin was surprised.

"Don't be so dense Justin," Jonah whispered as Emily made her way back to them.

"I'll take 'em both!"

Justin got more comfortable when they got to the park. Jonah found excuses to get up and walk away.

"You never listened to punk before Friday?"

Justin shrugged. "No, I totally had."

Emily cocked her head and smiled. Justin felt like he was melting. He knew she was trying to tell him it was OK.

Justin sighed. "OK, OK I never heard it before. It was cool though I like it."

"Wait to you hear *Minor Threat* it is not goofy, they are angry. They have a song called Screaming at a Wall it is totally about those jerks in the parking lot." Emily was smiling even when talking about the rednecks who harassed them. "I don't know it speaks to me."

Justin looked around the park. Jonah talked to a guy with a spiked Mohawk. A boombox sat at his feet, across the park they could faintly hear the beat. In the middle of the park, Electric Fred sat with his headphones on sketching in his notebook. Justin turned back to Emily. He was staring at her long enough to start to notice her birthmarks. She didn't seem to mind. Still, he had to say something.

"Uh, so probably more punks in California, bands, and stuff."

Emily's smile faded slightly.

"What's wrong? I'm sorry I shouldn't have brought it up."

Emily shrugged. "No, it is really cool there, I want to be excited it's just I am going to miss Bloomington, my old friends, new friends."

Justin nodded. He saw Emily's father pull up in his car in the parking lot. Emily turned and waved at her dad before holding up a finger for one more minute. She turned back to Justin. "Hey I only have few weeks before I go," She pulled out a pencil and tore a piece of paper out of the bag from the record store. She wrote down her number. "Call me OK."

Emily picked up her bag from Karma and took off running towards her dad's car. Jonah walked up behind him.

"If you don't call her. I'm kicking your ass."

CHAPTER EIGHT

Jonah waved to Justin as he skated past heading home. Justin was kicking up his skateboard when he saw Ray sitting on his front doorstep reading a comic book.

"Where you been?"

"Twenty-fifth. Dude, I didn't know you were coming."

Ray followed him around to the garage. Justin didn't have a key, just a four-digit code for the garage door.

"My family was being weird, I had to get out of the house."

They waited for the garage door. Ray went straight to the garage fridge that just like he did in their old house. It was filled with 7-ups and RC colas. He got himself an RC and threw one at Justin. Ray put the cool can on his forehead until they walked into the air-conditioned house. Justin sat on the couch and didn't move tired from skating to and from the comic store. He wasn't sure if he had a goofy smile on his face but he pulled out the paper with Emily's number on it and showed it to Ray.

Ray was surprised but just shook his head. "That's cool dude but did you hear me?"

Justin took a sip of his RC. "Your family is not that weird."

Ray looked pretty shaken.

Justin dropped his comics on the coffee table. "Why don't we look through some comics, maybe watch a movie…"

Ray shook his head. He was really disturbed. Justin felt bad about trying to change the subject. "Ok, what happened?"

Ray sighed. "My brother called me a f***** when I wouldn't play basketball with him."

"What? Joe?"

"That's not all he was standing in my doorway, but I heard him outside at the same time. My dad was super mean and took his side. Except I think he was asleep watching the Reds game. It was confusing. It was like there were two of them."

"Woah, Woah. You aren't making any sense." Justin sat down and opened his soda. Ray looked crazy in front of him. Joe being mean was one thing, they were brothers and they did stuff to each other all the time. Ray's Mother and Father were two of the nice people he had ever met.

"Something is really, really wrong Justin."

He was scared. The tone of his voice made Justin uncomfortable. They both jumped at the sound of the garage door. He knew it was his mother who was coming home.

"Look I know how it sounds," Ray looked worried. "My dad has never, not once talked to me that way."

The door opened and Justin's Mom stepped in and was surprised to see Ray sitting there. She pointed at him.

"Didn't I leave you with a different kid?" She put down her purse. "You know the super tall smart one with no common sense."

"Jonah went home Mom," Justin shrugged "Can Ray stay here tonight?"

Mom put down her books. He knew what she was thinking. Ray had been here two nights before. They would go through long phases at each other's houses during the summer. She smiled.

"You know I love you Ray but your folks want you at home for dinner now and then." Mom said as she went up the stairs to the main level of the house. "I am going to start charging rent to the both of you."

Ray breathed a deep sigh of relief. Justin didn't want to make him feel worse, he knew that Ray would have to go home at some point.

"You want to watch Big Trouble in Little China?"

Ray has dozed off and on through the movie. They had seen it enough times to know every one of Jack Burton's lines. Justin loved the movie just like he always did although he was looking through his comics. Ray's mind wondered to his father's face and how different it looked just moments apart. By the end of the movie, he was barely paying attention when the three storms appeared to protect Lo Pan the phone rang.

Justin ignored as he always did but a few seconds after the ringing stopped Justin's mom yelled down the stairs to the basement. "Justin! It's for you."

Ray looked at his friend who was confused. He had just seen Jonah and when he got phone calls it was almost always Ray or Jonah. Justin picked up the basement phone and yelled that he had it. He sat up straight in the chair and pointed at the TV.

He wanted the movie paused so Ray walked up to the machine and pushed stop.

"Hey Emily, no it's totally cool. We were just uh, yeah what are you up too?"

Ray watched Justin as he listened. He watched his friend's jaw slowly drop in disbelief that she was on the other end of the phone. They used to play Star Wars with her brothers in the old neighborhood. They all liked Emily. Her parents and Justin's parents were friendly. Justin mostly listened pumping his fist in excitement.

"Yeah, Totally I had fun."

"Totally," Ray whispered before putting his palm over his face.

Ray heard Justin's mother running down the steps. She whispered to Ray. "Who's the girl?"

"Emily McRoberts."

She didn't react. Justin waved them off bunching up the cord of the phone and trying to stretch it to the bathroom to get away from the audience. He pulled the cord under the door and shut it cutting them off. Ray picked up a pillow and threw it at the door.

"Not fair dude!" Ray laughed and turned to see Justin's mother. Her eyes moved right to left as if she was watching a Tennis match at double speed. Her body stayed still.

"Mrs. Morgan? Are you..."

She turned very slowly to look at Ray. Laughter came from the bathroom to slightly break the tension. Justin's normally friendly mother's face morphed into a cowl that twisted her features in an unattractive way. "What does that little slut want with my boy?"

Ray stepped back and fell on the couch. When he looked up Nicolette Morgan was no longer standing above him. Ray looked at the bathroom door. He inched up the stairs enough to peek. Mrs. Morgan was in the kitchen; she was at the stove stirring something. Ray gripped the banister, it was happening again. He looked back into the basement towards the TV.

"Justin saw her," he whispered. Ray ran to the bathroom door. He pounded on it. Justin opened the door and looked pale as a ghost.

"No, wait Justin please!"

"Emily, hold on a second." Justin put his hand over the phone. "Are you crazy dude?"

Ray nodded. "Maybe, did you see your mom down here before you went to the bathroom?"

Justin nodded. "See what?"

Ray hoped that was a sign that he was not crazy. Justin saw her too. He didn't imagine a raging bitch version of Mrs. Morgan. Justin pulled the door shut. He kept talking to Emily, he heard Justin laugh a few times. The quiet at first was a little nerve-wracking. Ray went over to the VCR and pushed play. The movie moved in front of him. He heard voices, saw the scenes but he felt disconnected. It was like something was creeping toward him. The worst part is he didn't know what.

Justin left the base of the phone at the bottom of the door where it was stretched to its full length. The twisty cord was stretched straight so he could sit on the toilet. He listened for a long time while they chatted. It was clear that Emily was lonely, needed someone to talk to.

"...I hated eighth grade; I mean the classes were fine. I got good grades it is just..."

It was strange for Justin to hear that Emily was as awkward about school as he and his friends were. To him, she glided through the halls like some beautiful fairy queen. He knew it was silly and he could never tell her that.

He felt it was time to say something. "I know the jocks and the rednecks. It is only going to get worse next year at least for us."

She paused on the other end for a moment. He didn't again, he brought California. "You know that is why the park is so cool?"

He knew what she meant. "People's Park?"

"Yeah, it is not just the punks. Look at Fred."

Justin was surprised to hear Emily bring him up. "Electric Fred?"

She laughed. "Poor Fred is mentally ill right, but it is a place he can go to. No one bothers him."

Justin felt bad thinking about Smiley yelling at him. No wonder the punks stood up for him. He just looked at him as a crazy old homeless guy. They knew him. They thought of him as ill, not crazy. Justin stood up to pace the small space the phone cord and the tiny bathroom allowed. He was basically able to nervously sway. He caught a glimpse of himself in the mirror and for a second, he looked different. Justin held his hand up in front of the mirror. The reflection of him didn't move.

Thunk, thunk, thunk! There was a pounding on the door. It was his mom; she must've needed the phone. Justin opened the door and saw Ray. He looked sweaty and pale. Justin pushed the door closed.

No, wait, Justin, please!" Ray put his foot in the door.

"Emily, hold on a second." Justin put his hand over the phone. "Are you crazy, dude?"

Ray nodded. "Maybe, did you see your mom down here before you went to the bathroom?"

Justin nodded. "See what?"

He slammed the door shut. Emily kept talking. He heard some of what she said but couldn't help looking at the mirror. His reflection stared back at him and suddenly he felt watched. In the background, he heard someone yelling on Emily's end. A voice called out her name.

"Hey my dad needs the phone; will I see you at the park?"

Justin smiled subconsciously; he knew she couldn't see it. He was about to say yes when he saw his reflection nod.

"Justin? You there?"

Deep breaths. He saw himself take deep breaths. The young man in the mirror was right again. He needed sleep. "Yeah, I'll see you there."

CHAPTER NINE

Justin rolled over in his bed and expected to see Ray in a sleeping bag on the floor. He sat up and stared at the bedroom door. Ray sat up his eyes locked on the clock. It was almost nine AM. The clock was fuzzy in his vision and the blinds kept the summer light out. Mom had let them sleep and there was a good chance she was working in her new office, to set it up.

"What are you doing?" Justin still sounded half-asleep.

Ray looked back at his friend. Justin had rarely seen fear in his friend's eyes. He looked scared.

"Mom is coming at nine to get me."

Justin fell back on the bed. He looked up at his wall. It was blank his old wall was filled with posters from horror and science fiction movies. He had one from ALIENS that was just above his old bed. Ripley facing off with the Alien, his mother hated that poster but his dad defended him. It had folded out off the cover of a Starlog movie magazine. He put it up because of the alien but he was looking more and more at Sigourney Weaver. He didn't miss his posters, he thought he just wanted a picture of Emily and he looked at the spot on the wall where he would put it...

"You don't even care."

Justin saw Ray gathering his things. He thought about the mirror and what he saw when he was on the phone. It had to be in his mind. This all had to be in Ray's mind too. Justin pushed the covers off and rubbed his eyes. He tried to think of something compassionate he could say but the reality was he thought Ray was being dramatic.

"Dude, just talk to your dad, I don't think he would ever talk to you..."

Ray was gone, he was out the bedroom door leaving it open. Justin watched him head to the front door where his shoes waited for him. He thought about following him, but he didn't like how pissy he was acting. He thought about yelling whatever but just scanned his room. The comic books had not all been read and organized.

The front door slammed as Ray left. It shook the tiny house. Justin got the message, but his mind was on Emily, she made it hard for his teenage mind to ponder anything else. He saw the tape his cousin made him was still in the tape deck. He searched for the band Emily talked about in the names written on the sleeve of the tape. Smiley's handwriting was terrible, his pen seemed to die in the middle of song titles. There at the start of the B side was *Minor Threat*—"Filler/ Don't wan a He r It."

He flipped the cassette and pushed rewind. He waited as it wound back all the way the start of that side. This was her favorite band and he couldn't wait to hear it. It snapped when it was done. He pushed play and waited. There was a needle drop and then the subtle snaps and pops of vinyl caught on the tape. Superfast bass. Snare building up and then the explosion. The voice "What happened to you? You're not the same..."

The rest of the words came and it and the song seemed over quickly. The beat was fast, the screams of anger throughout. Justin smiled. He loved the raw energy and loved that Emily liked it too. He left the tape playing blaring out of his room as he walked to the upstairs bathroom.

He stopped in front of the mirror. It was normal. He lifted his hand and the reflection matched. He felt stupid for even questioning it for a moment. He stared at himself, the mushroom top hair and the Hard Rock Café T-shirt. He thought about his two trips to the park. He just looked like any other dork from his school. He wished he could raid an older brother's closet like Jonah did stealing punk shirts. He couldn't look any more typical.

Justin leaned down and opened the cabinet. He wasn't sure it would be there. In the old house, he would have found them. The hair clippers waited for him. The case snapped open. Mom cut his hair his whole life, and his father too. One reason his Mushroom top got crazy was that she had not offered to cut it since the weekend before his father died.

She had cut his hair first and dad last. Justin stared at the blades and had the morbid thought. The tiny hairs left on the clippers. They were dad's hair. Justin felt a rush of sadness that morphed quickly into anger. He put his fingers on the last remaining part of his father and stared at his finger. Tiny hairs were all that remained of him. The sounds of some angry punk song drifted through the open door of his bedroom. He wished his father was here to do this. He gently put the tiny hairs on the counter and plugged in the clippers. He snapped on the clippers. It couldn't be that hard.

Just leave a line down the middle.

He started just over the ear. No guard and ran it through like he was mowing the lawn. The hair fell out in handfuls to the sink. He could see the skin on his head. Justin let out a deep breath. He was going for it now. He kept shaving. He stopped when he reached the half waypoint. It looked cool.

"Fuck yeah!"

It was that moment that he knew his hair had overtaken his father's hair on the counter. It was lost. Justin took a breath. He was not coming back. It was something he knew but a part of him never accepted it. All the love, support and teaching his father offered him in his 13 years of life was all over. He turned the clippers back on. The sound was the same but somehow to Justin, the clippers sounded angry this time.

He started on the other side; he gained confidence and now it went quicker. The Mohawk was almost complete, he could see it in the mirror. He would have heard his mom coming down the hall but the loud hum of the clippers so close to his ears drowned her out.

"What are you listening to and oh my god what have you done?"

He saw her in the mirror, her jaw close to the floor. He didn't care what she thought at all, he felt the waves of anger, embarrassment and even sorrow at seeing his hair cut into a hawk. He turned off the clippers with a snap.

Ray sat silently in the passenger seat of the truck as town gave way to cornfields and forested hills. His father was quiet. He expected his mother and had hesitated to get in the truck. Dad just smiled and waited while Ray thought about jumping on his skateboard. This looked like his father, his normal smiling happy father. He opened the door and took a seat.

"Have fun?"

Ray nodded but chose silence as his father put the truck in drive. They had on local radio coming out of Indianapolis. Ray didn't actually hear words. His father didn't speak until they hit the gravel drive that leads up to their house the woods swaying around them under a slight breeze.

"Something wrong son?"

He put the truck in park. Ray could get out and run to his room. He thought about it, but his father's voice sounded normal.

"Dad, why did you yell at me?"

"What? I didn't yell at you?" He pulled out his keys but stayed in the cab. "But if I did, I am sure you did something totally stupid."

Ray saw his brother on the little basketball court. He missed a shot and had to run towards the woods to chase down the rebound.

"Joe called me a faggot and you told me to go play ball and I just wanted to read in my room I was tired and..."

"Woah, woah if I yelled at anyone it would be that lunkhead." Dad pointed at Joe as he actually made a shot.

Ray wanted to tell him about how odd things were happening. How he was hearing people in more than one spot, seeing things, people in the wrong places. He wanted so badly to tell him, but he just couldn't see any response but them calling him crazy.

"I'm sorry I'm just tired," Ray said as he got out and ran towards his room. Joe yelled at him. He probably wanted him to come to play but Ray was inside before could get it out. His mother stood in the Kitchen. It stopped Ray. She held a kitchen knife in a shaky hand.

"Mom?"

Her eyes were blank, there was no greeting coming. Ray froze as she lifted her head slightly. The whites of her eyes were gone red swirled in them like Jupiter's clouds in fast forward.

Ray question it, he took the stairs in as few steps as he ever had. He slammed his door and moved his bed to block it. His breath was heavy in the silence of the room. He heard the thunk of the basketball. He heard the sound of the stairs creaking as someone or thing came up the stairs. They were trying to be quiet.

Outside Ray faintly heard the sound of his father's voice. It carried to his open window. He couldn't make it out but he heard his brother loud and clear.

"What? I didn't call him no faggot. That's bullshit Dad, I swear."

Footsteps were coming down the hall. Ray jumped on his bed and put his ear to the panel of the door and listened. He never noticed how cheap and thin his door was before. The footsteps stopped short of his door. Ray reached over to grab his aluminum baseball bat. He squeezed the grip tight and stepped back off the bed. The door handle turned. Whoever it was pushed the door, but the bed did the job of blocking.

"Ray sweetheart," It sounded like his mother speaking softly. "Dinner time."

It sounded like her but why did she try to open the door? And it was not even ten o clock in the morning.

"Not hungry," he yelled at the door.

"Boys! I got breakfast if y'all want it." Mom was yelling from the kitchen, her voice distant this time. Ray ran to the door and pushed the bed out of the way, the bat still in his other hand. He swung the door open. The hallway was empty. No Mom, no kitchen knife, no monster version of Dad or his brother. Ray closed the door and fell to his bed just wanting everything to be normal.

Fred wrote in the notebook; the last page was almost full. He spun the dial on his Walkman radio to 93.5 watching the white stick on the radio get to the safest spot away on the dial from any radio stations. Right in the sweet spot between Q95 and WBWB Bloomington's pop hit station. He was tired and had nothing left to say so he flipped the notebook around and began a drawing. He didn't know what it would be at first but it became a female symbol. He drew little eyes on it at the base.

"I see you," he said and closed it. It was full. The latest report was written and ready for submission. He probably should have dressed lighter. It was a hot summer day in the park. He had been sweating so much he had dripped on the pages causing some of the ink to run. He hoped prime Minster Chi-San would accept this notebook with his usual grace.

Fred had a feeling that the sun had lowered beyond the horizon. He heard the lights click on and start to buzz. He sensed the population of the park decrease. He didn't look at anyone, there was always a chance they would use telepathy to steal his soul and he couldn't allow eye contact during the daylight. He only looked at people inside where the plaster and concrete deadened the mental storm.

The young people had left. They had a swar-ay of some nature to distract them. In the corner of his vision, the black man who returned from Nam was asleep on the bench. His bottle was empty at his feet. In the distance, the traffic continued but Fred was alone in the park. He put today's notebook in his bag.

"Getting lazy Fred Curtis. This notebook is almost all drawings. Prime Minister Chi-San will not be happy no, sir."

The sunlight was gone, it seemed sudden. The summer heat was still strong, the humid air thick. Fred reached out and grabbed some of it. He was hungry and looked the way of the Coffee Shop. He could already taste the cheese sandwich. It was too hot. The flavor repelled him. He opened his hand and let the summer air run away. He watched it blend into the night and felt privileged to be able to see it.

"Ice Cream, good sir." He waved his finger at the sleeping vet. "Ice cream tonight and thank you for your service."

The Vet grumbled, coming close to opening his heavy eyelids. Fred grabbed his backpack and stumbled away before the man woke. He stopped in the middle of the park. The construction had stalled again. The hole they dug into the park remained empty and the promised sculpture never appeared. Fred stood still and stared into the hole. He had to make himself so still that he could pocket out of reality; remain unseen and still be able to gaze upon the park as if he was still there. His heart slowed, it was the only sound he heard, the soft beat of his blood being pumped. A keen traveler might be able to hear the beat and track him.

He was as invisible as he could be. He gazed down into the hole. They say they dug it for the sculpture but he knew better. The hole was always here, covered by dirt that could hardly be called earth. No, it was seething negative energy, not soil but radiating like a tiny collapsed star smack dab at the heart of this park. It was why he sat in this park watching it. The static from empty FM transmissions in his earphones blocked him from the mental assault.

It was impossible to tell how deep it was. He didn't think the city of Bloomington public works had the means to attain a hell scoop but this hole was mighty. The human eye saw four feet of depth but Fred knew it was an illusion.

If one stared into it for mere seconds, they would not see it. The forces of evil blend with darkness and void as naturally as we breathe. Fred stared long enough to see; they were like minnows. Not of flesh but of gold light. They had metallic teeth that cut the air leaving a floating trail of blood that most had no eyes to see.

Sick creatures. Hate-mongering beasts that hide in the void and feed on anger. They spill forth from this gateway into the air and find homes in the bodies of the weak-willed. They direct their anger and intolerance, and feed.

"I see you," Fred slid back out of the pocket and back into the universe. He was visible again, but he had to do it. He kicked dirt on the hole. There was plenty of loose dirt. He kept going until a police car pulled up on Kirkwood. It was too late to slip out of space-time. Not while being watched.

"What are you doing?" The cop yelled from his car. Fred saw him. His skin was not red but the disguise masked his horns. The Prime Minister could not afford for Fred to die in a hail of bullets from this agent of the void. Fred kept walking toward the sanctuary of the Jiffy Treat.

A car honked at him as he crossed Dunn Street. It wasn't his turn maybe. He was light-headed he needed two scoops of Butter Pecan or the mission was in danger.

Fred stopped in from of the large glass window at the Jiffy Treat. There was a young man flirting at the counter with Ericka, the Jiffy Treat woman. Fred waited to have the store to himself. He looked at his reflection. His hair looked different. He was not balding at the top. His hair was combed. In the reflection, he wore a sport coat. For a moment he thought the glass had turned to liquid. He touched it with his finger, and, like a disturbed pond, he watched it ripple out.

When the liquid glass cleared, he touched it again. This time it was solid. Now he saw the Fred he knew from the mirror. His bald head reflected the light from inside the store. His dress was a bit embarrassing in contrast. He never cared about that before. His appearance didn't matter, or it shouldn't. He was far enough from the hole, so he turned off the radio. He still heard the static echo faintly, and it was enough to protect him at this distance. Fred opened the door and the bell rung. Ericka said his name but Fred ignored her. He touched the inside of the window with a tap. Solid glass.

Fred sighed. "Butter Pecan please."

CHAPTER TEN

They kick flipped their skateboards up before they crossed the giant limestone gates that marked the entrance to campus from town. Justin looked down the length of Kirkwood Ave. It was filled with cars moving slowly east and west to cruise the strip. It was only six PM, but in the Indiana summer at the end of the Eastern Time zone, it was after nine before the sun started to disappear.

"Cruisers already?"

Jonah nodded and was first to cross the street. They skipped the spaceport. Emily was already supposed to be in the park waiting for them. Lucas and Jonah's brother were hanging by the Spaceport doors, a cloud of smoke hanging over them. The faint boombox sound of *The Damned* traveled over traffic. Jonah waved at his brother who ignored him.

When they turned the corner around the bike shop into the park Justin saw Emily right away. She sat with two older punks including Lisa the woman who yelled at them the other day. When she saw them, she stood up and ran to them. Justin was ready for a hug and got more excited than he should've but then she stopped.

"Woah, haircut." She reached up and rubbed the left bald side of his head. It was that moment that he remembered that Ian, the guy from *Minor Threat*, shaved his whole head. He wished for just a second that he had shaved the whole damn thing.

The older punk rocker sitting on the wall at the back of the park laughed. "Fresh cut!"

Justin felt a moment of embarrassment, but Emily smiled and erased all doubt. "I love it."

Jonah pointed at his generic IU dept of Education shirt. "We got to get you a matching outfit dude, you can't shop at the mall for that shit."

Emily smiled. "There are some pretty cool shirts at Karma."

Jonah pointed at the short wall in the front of the park. A couple skaters had their decks lined up against it and were perched there.

There was a punk kid, not much older than sixteen who looked as if he had not slept in a week. He was wearing a leather jacket; his hair was spiked like a cactus and he wore a spiked dog collar. He looked shabby except for a pair of fancy boots. He pointed to on his feet. "Yeah, I had to go to Future Shock in Indy to get these."

"Fuck that," Jonah pointed to his combat books whose sole he had worn down skateboarding. "Army-Navy store for $15."

"What's Future Shock?" Emily asked. Justin was glad she didn't know, he wanted to know but was embarrassed to ask.

The punk guy on the wall adjusted the spiked dog-collar around. "So, one of the dudes in *Toxic Reasons*..."

"They're a band from Indy," Jonah added.

"...owns a store. The only place south of Chicago where you can buy Doc Marten boots..."

"...shirts, spike collars."

They continued to talk about the store, but Justin lost focus. He looked down the length of the wall and saw Electric Fred, who also sat on the wall about ten feet down. Fred had his notebook on his lap and he stared at the center of the park. They walked past him and Justin could hear the blaring static. Fred didn't look up or seem to notice them. Justin wasn't sure the guy would remember their nasty confrontation at all.

They sat down on the wall. Justin heard the sound of *Bad Company* coming slowly down the road in the speakers of the Blue Chevy Nova. A truck behind it was playing *AC/DC's* Shook Me All Night Long, and they were doing a sonic battle. It sounded awful as both sets of speakers were being pushed beyond any acceptable limits. The combination of static and songs was beyond awful.

"Hey that's him," Emily pointed at the Nova.

"Yeah, my brother says folks call him Supercruiser, cuz' he cruises up and down the strip almost all the time. He just works at Burger King long enough to get gas money. Some people think he lives in his car."

They all laughed. They talked about music for a long time. Super cruiser came back around four times, once even listening to *RATT*'s song *Round and Round*. They all laughed at the irony. Justin looked up to see Fred past Emily's shoulder. He kept his eye on the mentally ill man just in case. He worried a little bit. The man just kept writing in his notebook.

Jonah got up to talk to his brother who now arrived with Lucas to the Park. Bro didn't want to deal with a younger brother. He seemed embarrassed and annoyed that we were here. Lucas sat at the back of the park clearly flirting with Lisa. Jonah almost instantly turned around to walk back.

"Thanks for meeting me tonight, I just couldn't stay at home." Emily leaned back on the wall.

"No sweat, I wanted to see you." Justin smiled.

"Me too, I wanted to see you," Jonah smiled knowing he was being a fifth wheel. He thought it was funny. "You guys are so stoked I am here."

"I actually am," Emily shrugged. She hesitated and looked around the park as if she didn't want to be heard. "My family is being weird."

Justin only knew her dad around the old neighborhood, but he seemed nice enough. You never know, he could be a drunk. The thing is, you hear rumors like that. "Your dad has always been cool to me. What is he doing?"

"Just being mean. He is never like that but today he was saying just awful things."

Justin thought about Ray and how he had dismissed his concerns.

"You think I'm crazy."

Jonah nodded yes. But Justin shook his head. "No way. Ray said the same thing, that his brother and his parents were being mean and intolerant." He left out the part about seeing them in two places at once.

"Ray's parents?" Jonah laughed "That's crazy, they put up with my bullshit better than anyone. They're super nice."

"He said his dad called him a f*****."

"Ray's dad?" Jonah laughed out loud. "Billy Smith called him a f*****. No way, his pop is like Bill Cosby; a complete and total goody-two-shoes."

"Maybe it was his brother, but I don't understand why he was mad with Ray over it. Something like that. Just not like him."

Justin looked up and Fred was right behind Emily. She jumped; he didn't move. He had an eye-brow raised, and one headphone off. The static was loud.

"Hey, Fred how are you?" Emily said.

"They feed off hate you know, they come straight up out of the ground. Demons unleashed from a realm not unlike hell. It is not in the earth but by god the red-hot core of this planet is like a door. They slip under the crack at the bottom of the door you see, right under it!"

"Come on shut the..." Jonah looked across the park and saw Lucas and his brother watching them. Jonah leaned back.

"They act different because they feed off us; use that anger and hate as fuel."

A truck almost as tall a monster truck passed at the same time. A man in the passenger seat holding a soda from Hardees pointed at Justin. "Nice hair cut! Look Ricky, it's a f***** I****! That's you right, Indian f**?" The woman crammed in the middle of the truck and Ricky, the driver, laughed.

Jonah stood up, taller than any thirteen-year-old should ever be. He didn't seem scared at all. "Fuck you redneck. You know that big truck doesn't make up for your little penis."

The Hardees cup was half full when it hit the wall behind Jonah who stepped out of the line of fire just in time. The truck stopped; Ricky put it in park in the single lane. Both thick jock-redneck hybrids got out and ignored the honks from the cars behind them as they stopped in traffic. Justin grabbed his skateboard by the trucks, Emily jumped on the sidewalk beside him.

"You see now? Agents of the Void, that is who they become," said Fred. "They circle this spot collecting spores in their blood. They hate you rebels who clean your brains with that blaring nonsense you call music. You are their natural enemies."

Justin didn't really hear him. He was focused on the huge asshole in the Bloomington South varsity Football T-shirt coming at him.

"Come on Steve-O," Ricky said as he came around the truck.

All the punks in the park ran forward to help, but they didn't need to because Justin swung his skateboard at Steve-O. The metal trucks hit the side of his head knocking him back into his friend Ricky.

One of the punks jumped over the short wall and punched Ricky. The honking got louder. The Woman in the truck yelled at the guys to get back in. Justin looked up and saw a tiny face caked in foundation make-up and surrounded by a corona of bleached blonde hair.

"Get back in the truck!" she yelled.

Ricky pulled his friend back. Jonah held his fists up like an old-timey boxer. Emily pulled at Justin's arms. Ricky yelled as they struggled to climb backwards into the high truck. "You're dead, all you fucking freaks. This is war you freak motherfuckers."

Ricky looked up from the ground beside his truck and saw a crew of punks who looked nine feet tall with the help of the wall. The older punks were lined up. Lucas crossed his arms. "You started this bullshit, but bring it if you want."

Zoe, the homeless vet, had dropped the bottle he held and stumbled towards the way. "Get your cracker asses out of my fucking park," he slurred.

Ricky and Steve-O climbed up into the truck and peeled away.

CHAPTER ELEVEN

Fred watched the confrontation from afar. He knew it would happen eventually. The agents of the void circled the park every night to guard the hole. He sat at the end of the wall and watched. He had bought the little make-up mirror at the Salvation Army and it had been his secret weapon ever since.

He held it at the right angle to watch the fight in the reflection. The young man named Ricky moved at two different speeds in the different realms. The reflection caught the version of Ricky moving faster, pulling his body to attack, even if he didn't want to do it the void pushed him to act. The barrier between worlds was thin here, near the gateway.

Fred opened his notebook to the last page and drew as the fight went on behind him. He sketched a picture of the truck. He wrote a last heartfelt plea to Prime Minister Chi-San as the fight appeared to break up. He closed the notebook and walked down the street. Part of him sensed the sun going down and the street lights flickering on around him.

Fred got to the Jiffy Treat and turned off his headphones. He still heard the buzz in his ears. He looked at the cars and trucks creeping slowly up and down Kirkwood Ave. He turned back to the glass window of the Jiffy Treat. This humid night the store was packed with a line out the door.

He could see the street behind him in the reflection, but it wasn't cars he saw. Tanks, dragons, and canons being pulled on wheels. The void was just the modern Archons who hid their armies in a veil of normality that he could see through, like a crystal-clear pane of glass. He needed the reflection to help, but he saw. He turned to the crowd of agents lined up at the ice cream shop, some with the nerve to wear the skin of young boys and girls. Fred walked along the line forcing himself into their line of sight making sure he made eye contact with everyone in the line.

"I see you! Filthy Archons!" Fred shook with rage. Many of the people in line were scared, and they should've been. One of the agents in adult skin yelled at him to leave. Fred didn't hear his words. He held up his mirror and pointed to it.

"Just words you void fucking shit-bird!" Fred shook as he backed away nodding. "I see, oh yeah I see." He needed to get the notebook to the Prime Minister, but he was hungry and tired.

He walked the alley that cut across the block back to the Spoon. Once the doors to the coffee shop opened the sound of jazz and the light hit him. Fred walked to counter. Lisa met him with his Coke and cheese sandwich. Her pitch-black hair was teased up. Her make-up looked like an Egyptian queen prepared to be mummified. He looked at the sandwich and then her.

"Are you Lisa? I mean really Lisa."

She nodded, but Fred didn't relax until he held up the mirror. She smiled at her own reflection. Fred saw only her. He snapped the mirror shut and grabbed his sandwich.

"You're an angel my dear."

Fred fought with the keys to the apartment every time. The dead-bolt turned, and he thought it was open, he would push, and have to turn the key a little more to open it. He pushed the door open and the stacks of old newspapers slowed his progress. He dropped his radio on a stack of books on a table inside the door. Every inch of the apartment had things. Mostly notebooks;

the prime minster copies them and returned them always. He had a stack of notebooks for every year since he started writing them on March 18th, 1974.

He went to his bedroom. The cat who was supposed to live in the apartment across the courtyard was purring on his bed. He knew she crawled in the bathroom window. He used to chase her out but he liked hearing the sound of her purring. He never fed her and each morning he put her back out.

He went to his nightstand. He opened the drawer. He had to keep it empty or the transmission would not go through. He left a nickel in there once and in the morning his notebook was blank, he never knew if the transmission went through and lost a day of work. He kept a mirror inside a picture frame propped above it. He had to see his reflection to know that he was not compromised before he transmitted each notebook.

He placed it in the drawer and prayed. He had to have faith. The Prime Minister couldn't tip his hand to the Void. If he responded it could shine a light on their connection. He had always assumed it was some form of advanced teleportation. Unable to transmit biological information, the notebooks would have to do.

Fred closed the notebook and placed it in the drawer.

"Godspeed," He whispered and pushed it shut. He would not risk breaking the connection before morning.

Fred laid down and fell instantly to sleep.

CHAPTER TWELVE

Fred jumped up in bed when the door swung open. The dream he was having disappeared and it was like his bedroom was filled with smoke left behind. He woke up like people did in movies, his breath labored. The cat jumped up and hissed. He looked at the open door and it was no surprise who came in. He looked around and saw no one. She was hiding.

"Where are you?" Fred asked through his breath labored. "I'm going to find you, and when I do..." He looked at the window, the sun was just climbing. It was still early, he looked to the left of the bed and found no one hiding.

"I'm going to grab you and I'm going to..."

Fred dropped his head over the corner of the bed and looked under. There she was, stuffed in a space only her 10-year-old self could go. Bright piercing blue eyes got wide when he saw her.

"...Tickle you to death!" Fred reached under the bed and the young girl laughed, as she squirmed away from his reach. She rolled out on the other side. Fred rolled on top of the bed and reached down to tickle her as he had threatened.

"Anaka!" a voice called from the kitchen. "Come on you two. Breakfast time."

Anaka waited at the door smiling. "Come on dad, chase me!"

She was gone, but Fred Curtis was still being held to the bed by an invisible murk of sleep that worked like extra gravity. "Just give me a minute sweet pea."

Fred looked at the ceiling. Catherine and Anaka laughed in the kitchen and he was certain it was the most beautiful sound in the universe. He knew about the universe too; it was hyperbole but at least he understood the scale he was talking about. He put his feet on the floor and looked at his socks laying there. They were right near his feet, but they felt like a mile away when he calculated the effort involved in reaching them. Jupiter started climbing the horizon.

His nightstand drawer was opened. He thoughtlessly pushed it shut as he reached for the socks. He grunted, feeling old as a redwood. When he sat up, he felt accomplished but the drawer cracked back open. That was odd. He just pushed it shut and it slowly rolled open like something pushed it from the inside.

Fred opened it this time. There was a notebook he had never seen before. 40 pages, single-spaced wide ruled. He pulled it out of the drawer and opened it. His handwriting filled the page, he turned the page, and again he saw his unique handwriting. He didn't remember writing in any notebook like this. He had a legal pad on his desk but used his Apple to type most of his notes up. Page after page was filled with words. His words. Drawing in a style he had not used since doodling in his undergrad days.

Fred turned back to the first page. It started with a sentence written in bold letters. THE NOTEBOOKS OF 1983 ARE COMING TRUE. Fred walked over to his chair and sat down to read.

"Fred, are you coming to breakfast?" Catherine called from downstairs.

He didn't answer. He just read. Before long he had read half of the pages in the notebook. They were rambling. Addressed to the Prime Minister of China. They talked of shadow people who worked as agents for an evil force called the Void. It was terrifying because Fred couldn't escape three facts: It was beside his bed and in his handwriting but he didn't remember writing it.

On the last page there was a note. "If you find this notebook it belongs to Fred Curtis, please acknowledge the contents and return it to the transmission drawer." He looked at his watch. He had been up late at the observatory as it was the first clear night in weeks. It was possible he was overly tired.

He thought this was over. The strange lag in the reflections, the occasional shabby version he saw looking back at him in the occasional puddle, or storefront window. He wrote something in the notebook and pushed it back in the cabinet.

"What's wrong?"

Catherine stood in the doorway. As beautiful as the day they met. He jumped up and gave her a kiss. She was surprised.

"No really?" Catherine blushed. "I mean, I like it. But what is the occasion?"

He smiled and walked past her and he hoped she didn't see him close the drawer.

The cat jumped off the bed waking Fred up. He never even made it under his cover. He thought he heard the sound of the nightstand drawer closing. He never saw anyone return it. They were either quick, or as he originally thought, perhaps it was beamed like Star Trek to the destination.

Fred put his feet down and watched the cat jump up on his toilet and crawl out the window. He turned to look at the piles of his oldest notebooks that he kept in the bedroom.

The 70s. He didn't understand what was happening then. Not even close. So he found it hard to read those.

He opened the drawer. He picked up yesterday's notebook and walked out of the bedroom to file it with the current stack. He was sleepy still and dropped it on the floor.

It fell open to the last page.

PLEASE STOP WRITING. NO MORE NOTEBOOKS.

It was his handwriting. He knew he didn't write that before. Fred turned back to look at the nightstand. He closed the one in his hand and dropped on the completed pile.

"Interesting." He walked to the pile of empty notebooks that he got from Kroger when his SSI check came in. Buying notebooks was the first stop before paying off his tab at the Spoon and Jiffy Treat.

He opened the empty notebook and put it in his backpack. Today would be an interesting day, an interesting notebook.

CHAPTER THIRTEEN

Ray hadn't left his room in hours. He didn't turn on the music, kept everything quiet so he could listen to what the rest of his family were doing. He tried to read but the comic books just sat on his lap and he listened to sounds that came from beyond his door.

He was used to the sound of the TV. Normally he would faintly hear the sounds of baseball this time of year or his mother watching *Donahu*e. He didn't know what he was hearing, but it sounded like it might be construction. He heard pounding, things breaking. It was like the house was being torn apart. He wanted to go to Justin's house; anything to get away.

Ray slowly opened the door. The closest phone in the house was in his parents' room. He could see the phone by their bedside, but it felt a hundred miles away. He had to pass the top of the stairs. He took a deep breath and told himself that all the sounds were coming from downstairs.

He took off towards his parents' room as fast as he could. He didn't stop at the top of the stairs. He only got a flash of what was happening below. Joe stood at the bottom of the stairs unmoving but staring up at him. Ray's heart raced faster, it felt like the air was sucked out of the house. He ran past the door and had to turn around and slam it.

He didn't see Joe, but he felt like he was there. Ray leaned on the door feeling oddly winded, his heart raced. He looked straight down when he saw the light under the door disappear. Something blocked it. Ray twisted the lock and backed towards the phone.

Ray kept his eye on the door, even as he picked up the phone. He didn't need to look to dial Justin's number. The commotion downstairs stopped as he waited through a second and third ring.

"Come on pick up, pick up," Ray whispered.

Justin answered.

"Thank God, dude," He whispered. "I need to come over."

Justin paused. "My mom is being weird too, it's crazy. Emily said the same thing about her folks."

"Please dude, I got to get out of here."

"Yeah, come over."

"Can your mom come to get me?"

"I don't know. I gotta ask but dude she is being weird too..." Justin paused. "I'll call you back..."

"No, I can't hang up."

"OK hold on," Justin put down the phone. Ray heard him yell for his mom. He waited and heard a sound from the master bathroom. Ray spun to look. His mother stood in the dim light of the bathroom. Her face was covered by shadow. He didn't expect her to be here.

"Mom?"

She tilted her head in a way he never saw her do before. "Were you planning on asking me?"

Ray didn't know what to say and froze. "Yeah, I just..."

"Hang up the phone."

"Mom I..."

She pointed and screamed as her face turned beet red. "Now!"

Ray slammed the phone on the cradle. He felt trapped. Afraid of what was on the other side of the door. They had changed. He thought of *Invasion of the Body Snatchers*. He had seen both versions on Sammy Terry's show. This wasn't his mother. Something had taken her, taken his father and brother. He didn't know if it was evil spirits or aliens. He knew how crazy it was.

"To your room, now!"

Ray opened the door and his father stood there. He moved aside for him in a strange, almost robotic motion. This wasn't his father.

Joe was at the top of the stairs. It was his brother's body, but it wasn't him. Ray got to his room and shut the door. He positioned the bed. He heard the phone ringing. Justin was calling back. No one answered the phone.

"Please come to get me," he whispered over and over.

Justin walked downstairs. "Hey, Mom."

He was about to yell at the punk singer level when he saw her in the kitchen. She stood at the sink staring at her faded reflection in the window. She had been doing dishes but seemed frozen.

"Mom?" Justin took a step back when she looked at him. Not the mom at the sink, only the faint reflection in the window looked at him. Justin stepped back. By the time he looked up, the sun beamed through the window and the reflection was gone. Still, his mom had not moved; didn't even blink at the bright light in her eyes.

"Woah, Mom are you okay?"

She turned slowly to look at him. "What do you need, honey?"

The request to go pick up Ray was on the tip of his tongue, but now he just wanted to get away.

"Nothing," He took off back to his room. He was so glad his mom agreed to put a phone jack in his room. He shut his door and heard the phone making a horrible sound. Ray had hung up on the other end. "No!" he yelled. He hung it up long enough to get the dial tone and dialed his friend's number.

He waited as the phone rang, nervously tapping the phone. The machine picked up.

"You've reached Bill…

"And Sarah…"
"And Ray…"
"Joe."
"LEAVE A MESSAGE!" they all yelled together as a family.

At the beep, Justin didn't know what to say. "This is Justin for Ray, uh call me back dude."

Justin cursed and dialed Jonah's number. The phone rang and rang.

"They always stare, and they feel the need to say something just because we are different."

Jonah walked out of the Spaceport arcade and held the door for his friend Robert. Jonah held his skateboard; Robert had a BMX bike locked up over by the record store.

"Welcome to my world," Robert said.

Jonah talked about how the punks got picked on all the time. Robert didn't understand. He dressed normal. He looked normal. Even if he said he understood, Jonah raised an eyebrow as they walked.

"For real, you don't get it?" Robert stopped. "How many black folks are in our neighborhood? Or in middle school, who was black besides me and Latonya?"

Jonah never thought much about the fact that there were only two black kids in their school. Bloomington was a liberal college town so all the parents he knew taught their kids not to think about race. Jonah also knew the town was surrounded by Indiana.

"I don't know anyone who is racist, dude. Not in Bloomington."

Robert laughed. "Plenty of people think they're not, sometimes it just a look, or weird behavior I mean Justin's parents are super nice. Sometimes too nice."

"So, is it like that all the time for you?" Jonah felt guilty.

Robert kept walking. "Yeah, only I can't choose to dress in a way to avoid it. I always look out of place here."

"I mean there are some backwoods mother fuckers at school."

"School is the worst."

Jonah stopped. Things have felt weird lately. "OK I admit I didn't see it, but it just feels like it is getting worse, doesn't it?"

"You just have your eyes open right now."

They stopped in front of the record store. Jonah pointed to the door.

"Really?" Robert laughed. "You ain't gonna spend it at 25th?"

"I can read Justin's comics," Jonah pulled on the door.

"You can listen to your brother's records."

Jonah was surprised when he didn't see Whittaker standing behind the counter. Tom the Hippie mostly stayed back in the office trying to mask the weed smell while Whittaker actually ran the store. Jonah walked straight to the punk 7-inch singles. He had spent a lot of time in this shop and rarely saw the manager who looked like a mountain man, complete with the graying beard. When he had seen the guy, he had a goofy smile. That was gone from his face now.

Jonah walked back to the section where the punk records were. The shelves were empty. He walked over to the used tapes. The metal and punk section looked empty. Robert was over in CD's. He knew that Whittaker took time off, and was in a couple bands, but he couldn't imagine the store without him.

All the good stuff appeared to be gone. Whittaker had put years of work into building the Punk/Hardcore/Metal section. How could he let this happen?

"Hey, Whittaker around today?"

"He's gone," Tom said.

"When will he be back?"

Tom stared past Jonah at Robert. It was weird; he had a laser focus on Robert. He followed Robert with his eyes from the moment they walked in.

Robert put up his hands and walked out. "Was just looking, you honky ass hippie."

Jonah walked to the counter. "He has money you know. He doesn't have to steal shit! That was messed up."

Tom the Hippie didn't react.

"When will Whittaker be back? What happened to the punk records?"

Tom the Hippie looked Jonah up and down. "He doesn't work here anymore. Might I suggest A Jimmy Buffet record?"

"What?"

"The Allman Brothers are pretty great. Much better than that noisy shit."

Jonah just walked out. Robert was unlocking his bike.

"Hey that was fucked up," Jonah tried to get in his path, but before he could move, Robert was gone. "Hey, let's just go to the park and..."

Jonah got on his skateboard and turned around to head towards the park.

Justin didn't even get a chance to say hello.

"Meet me at the park," Emily sounded desperate on the other side of the phone. "Soon as you can."

"What is happening?"

Emily lowered her voice. "My parents are not being themselves. Please just come to help me."

"I'll meet you at People's Park."

Justin hung up the phone and grabbed his skateboard. It wasn't normal for him to leave the house without one of his friends. He was only starting high school next year and his mom still had a habit of treating him like a baby.

He walked downstairs. Thirty minutes had passed, and his mother had not moved. The same dishes were in the sink.

"Mom?"

"Yes, dear." She didn't turn or look at him. He didn't think she would be cool with him just going to hang out at a park filled with weirdos. He didn't want the questions about Emily. Lastly, he didn't know what was wrong with her.

"I'm meeting Jonah for a movie."

She didn't react. Justin turned towards the door. He was on his board before it went shut behind him.

CHAPTER FOURTEEN

IN THE SUMMER, THE sun was not totally down till after 9 p.m., in Indiana Ray wanted to at least make it to the edge of town before it got dark. He knew it would be two miles on that two-lane country road before he would even see a sidewalk.

Being on those roads after dark was not just dumb, but dangerous. The highways were littered with dead critters. He took his sheets and a towel and tied them together into a makeshift rope. Once he tied it to his bed stand and hung it out the window, it made it most of the distance to the empty basketball court below. He would have to jump a little, but it was better than going through the house.

His brother was still awake, doing some kind of construction. He wasn't staying around to find out what it was. He carefully took out the screen and set it next to his bed, and threw the sheet-towel lifeline out the window. It hung just under the ten-foot height of the basketball rim. He would have to swing himself over to try and land on the grass. He threw his backpack to the ground, first.

The act of crawling through his window was scarier than he expected. It seemed a million miles to the ground. It looked so easy when Batman and Robin were climbing down the sides of the building on TV. Each second lasted forever and made Ray feel like he was dying. As soon as he was free from the window, he felt like he was falling; the sheet slid through his hands and it felt like they were on fire. When he caught the towel part he swung and awkwardly jumped. He thumped on the grass and wondered for a minute what he had broken.

"Fuck," Ray whispered as he slowly got up. He could see the shed where his bike was and knew he only had 25 yards to walk. The problem was, he would be in full view from the house.

Ray grabbed his backpack and ran to the corner. He looked around and didn't see anyone. He heard the racket from inside the house. It was as loud as if he was inside. They had the front door open.

Ray walked carefully to avoid branches or anything that would make a loud noise. He glanced back at the house. Inside the window was an unearthly glow. It lit a fire in Ray. He moved as quickly as he could without making a sound. It sounded like saws and hammers. They took his family and now they were destroying his house.

He ran into the shed and pulled the door open when he heard a voice.

"You! Stop!"

Ray turned expecting to see his brother. It was his voice. Something else was coming down the steps. It had as many legs as a spider, but his brother's body was connected where a head should be and he looked like a strange minotaur. His brother's eyes burned red and his head was crowned by two, sharp, upturned horns.

Ray screamed as he opened the shed and grabbed his bike. The brother creature closed the space in seconds carried by all those legs. Ray kicked the shed door expecting it to hit the monster. The door swung around and closed with a loud thump. The creature was not there, but the sound of the door against the shed was loud enough to be heard inside.

Now his father stood on the porch. He called his name, but Ray was on the bike already. He peddled against the resistance of the gravel on the road. but he went faster when he went to the grassy middle strip. Behind him, he heard his father's truck surge to life.

Ray turned off to a path he had ridden on his bike a thousand times that he was sure his father didn't know. He pedaled as hard as he could. Maybe the thing that took his father knew the path or could sense his body temperature.

He didn't know, he just pumped his legs as hard as he could. He heard the sound of his dad's truck go past. He heard his name called again, but he had to get to Justin. There was no time to think.

When he got to county highway 446, the only path to town, he waited until his dad drove past him. He waited ten minutes hiding in the grass until his dad's truck drove past again. He couldn't see who or what was behind the wheel, but once it was back on his driveway again, he pushed his BMX on to the shoulder of the highway and pedaled.

Just pedal.

Fred looked at the drawer. The notebook had been in there for two hours since he got home. Normally he waited till morning, hoping that would be enough time for the information to be read on the other side. Things had changed knowing the notebooks were not going to China, but to another Fred Curtis.

He knew a watched pot hardly ever came to boil, but as he sat there, he saw the drawer rattle. It moved.

He left only a brief note and the top of the blank page and asked for a reply: *Dear being claiming also to be Fred Curtis. Explain yourself.*

Fred opened the drawer and pulled out the notebook. Just as he expected the page had been filled.

Dear other Fred,

Sorry about the harsh tone of our last communication. I have long tried to ignore the reality I knew to be true. Cosmology is my field. As such, I have spent hours trying to understand the physical universe and how it works in the heavens beyond this earth. Since the first moments, the universe has been expanding. Considering what this means...the expansion of billions upon billions of light-years. Each nanoparticle is involved in this expansion, and some particles expand with great speed, others expand slowly.

This is how the universe expands in all directions of reality. It expresses itself in time, in space and in perception.

You and I are both Fred Curtis. We are Fred Curtis in two dimensions. I can't warn you enough that even the act of communication between our worlds is dangerous. But it shouldn't affect anyone but ourselves. Please other Fred. Guard your sanity and do not bridge our worlds again.

Our world is not run by hate as you fear. Our world is no closer to the apocalypse than yours. You are correct that we are sending so-called agents to change things.

    That was it. Fred closed the notebook. It was his handwriting, that much he could tell, but it was slightly neater.

Justin flew through the university campus that was largely empty for the summer. The last downhill before campus meant the town was red brick and hard on his skateboard so he walked the last bit. He put the punk rock mix his cousin made into his Walkman but the tape stopped mid-song. The little foam pads on the headphones were soaked with sweat. Justin pulled the Walkman out of his pocket and saw the first side of the tape had ended.

He looked ahead and saw Jonah crossing Kirkwood Ave towards the park. He put the cassette player in his backpack and walked the rest of the way. The music and the act of thrusting the skateboard took his mind away for a moment. It was all impossible. Why were their parents acting weird? What had happened to them?

There was a movie he had on VHS, taped off HBO, that came to his mind. *Invaders from Mars*, where the whole town was replaced by aliens starting with this old teacher. Jonah thought it was stupid, but he couldn't help thinking about it now. He knew they were not being invaded by Martians, but he also couldn't explain what was happening.

The park was loaded with people when Justin came around the corner. Both ice cream shops had lines out the door. The wall along the front of the park was crowded with young people sitting and hanging out.

Lucas and the older punks were holding court at the back of the park. Zoe looked wildly out of place as he was always telling a story. The night was young, but he had his drink in a paper bag and his Veteran hat.

"There are dudes that stayed over there. Black power motherfuckers who married locals and went native. Every time some racist motherfucker comes at me, I think, shit...I should've stayed..."

A punk rocker everyone called Bird passed out flyers. He was wearing motorcycle boots, a cowboy hat and spike bracelets, and he walked the park putting a small flyer in everyone's hand. Justin grabbed one. It was for a punk show in the guy's basement later that night. It said SAVAGE HOUSE on the flyer.

Jonah turned when he saw him. He looked as freaked out as he was. Emily appeared at the back of the park. Justin didn't see her walk up. She began to run when she saw him. Justin dropped his skate in the grass just in time for the hug. She squeezed him tight and for a moment everything stopped. She whispered over his shoulder. "Thank God, you're here."

"I'm here too," Jonah shrugged.

Emily pulled Justin over to a picnic table and waved to Jonah to follow. He knew she was scared so it seemed an odd moment to compliment her on her hair. Her long blonde lock had been half-dyed green. They all sat on the table together. Someone had drawn a huge "ST and Skate Punx" with a thick black marker where Justin sat.

"My mom is being weird," Justin said. "Ray thinks his parents and brother are trying to kill him. Emily?"

She nodded. "My parents are saying weird, hateful things."

Jonah nodded. "It is not just the parents; we were just at Karma. All the punk and metal records are gone. The old hippie dude fired Whittaker and was super racist to Robert."

"What?" Emily shook her head. "He was always like a happy stoner guy."

"Not now. He is jerky Klan guy now. I mean, why would he get rid of all the punk records? What is the reason for that?"

Justin was about to tell him it was fucked up. He never got the chance. There was a sound like thunder but the sky was a clear purple at dusk. He looked to the back of the park where three muscle cars had stopped in a line in the alley. The doors opened and a half a dozen Indiana stereotypes walked out. It was the rare combo of redneck and jock that the small towns in the southern tip of Monroe County bred. A sharp contrast to the sons and daughters of professors who mostly populated this park. They had stepped up to the sanctuary for weirdos with bad intentions.

It took a moment to remember the name, but he knew Ricky's face right away. He was the guy he had pummeled with a skateboard. One eye was swollen shut and purple, the good eye filled with anger. He pointed right at Justin.

Lucas stood up, and Jessie, the guy who looked like his cousin, Smiley, next to him was at the center of the group.

The biggest of the redneck group stepped out of a 1968 GTO wearing a shirt with an eagle clutching a confederate flag. His hair was long at the shoulder but trimmed perfectly in line with his eye-brows at the top

"Fuck, That's Kevin Buyers," Jonah whispered.

"Who?" Emily asked.

He was notorious. Jonah had heard his brother talk about him since they were younger. "He's a nineteen-year-old senior that hates all the skaters and punks."

Buyers pointed at Justin and waved him over. Justin shook his head.

"Oh no Freak, you put a whoppin' on my cousin. That shit don't fly, as long as I have a say."

Jessie the skinhead took a step forward. "This park is our space, numb-nuts. Get back in your dick-enhancing muscle cars and go."

Buyers laughed. He wasn't scared; the six dudes were all pretty big, all in shirts cutoff to show their arms. No matter how tough they thought they were, they were outnumbered. Then Zoe stoodup. Because he was always sitting and drinking it was easy to forget that Zoe was a monster; naturally strong, and tall. He also had the stare of a man who chased Viet-Cong across the jungle and, when drunk enough, once admitted to fragging an officer with a hand grenade when his platoon didn't like his orders.

At Zoe's side, stood a guy who looked every bit as big as them but with a long bangs skater haircut. He was busting out of a shirt that said "Cro-mags" with nuclear blast on it. He was as scary looking as any of those rednecks.

Buyers laughed again and looked at Zoe. "Look, the freaks got themselves a n*****."

Zoe threw his bottle at him. The glass thumped on Buyers' chest and didn't break until it hit the ground. It was like two armies coming together. Justin grabbed his skateboard and ran forward lifting it like a sword. The guy in the Cro-mags shirt went right at Buyers, punching him so hard he fell back on the hood of his car. Lucus took a punch that knocked him backwards. Zoe had someone in a headlock. Justin swung his skateboard which kept Ricky away. He knew better.

Justin felt anger swell in him, and he just wanted to lash out. He swung his deck at the back window of the GTO. The glass shattered. When he looked around, the rednecks were scrambling for their cars. Kevin Buyers was trying to get up, spitting blood and teeth in the alley.

Jonah and Emily were pulling on Justin. Everyone in the park scattered, not wanting to wait for the police. Justin turned around and the muscle car was gone. He saw three dragons in the alley and they snarled above a giant Orc who was trying to get to his feet, his mouth dripping blood. Justin screamed. Jonah pushed him harder to stand.

Justin blinked and they returned to normal. He thought he had seen their true form for a moment.

"Did you see that?"

Judging from the look on Emily and Jonah's faces they saw it, too. They saw all of it, and they ran as fast as they could. The problem was, Kirkwood Ave was now filled with tanks instead of cars. Each was topped by a monster who was hissing at them. They turned back toward the alley and ran towards the Coffee shop where they stopped. They were all breathing heavily.

"I think we saw their true form," Justin whispered.

"Whose true form?" Jonah had his hands on his hips.

"Whatever is taking over this town." Emily nodded.

Jonah shook his head. "What are we going to do?"

Justin held up the flyer for the punk show in the basement. "We get help."

When Lisa walked in for her shift at the Spoon, she found a flyer for a show tonight at the Savage house in her smock. Her co-worker Melissa had already hung up her smock and was putting up her hair when Lisa walked past her. With her hair up, you could see the part she had shaved underneath.

"You going to Savage tonight?"

She looked at the flyer. With Authority and GoManGo were playing. Two local bands, she had seen more times than she ever cared to, but there was a new band from Chicago called Gear. She shook her head at Melissa.

"I did what dishes I could babe, you catch the show, I gotta go study, but I might show up.." Melissa smiled and was out the back door of the former-house-turned- coffee-shop. There was no line waiting; it was a slow summer night. Only two customers were sitting with empty plates and cups of coffee that could use a refill. She first went to the tape deck and stopped the jazz mix. She pulled out her favorite Siouxsie and the Banshees album from her bag.

Lisa was just finishing the refills and putting the coffee back when the door swung open violently. She was about to yell to the person to cool it, but she looked up and saw Fred. He was a mess even for him. He didn't have on a sweatshirt or a button-up over his onesie suit. He had flip-flops on, and it was clear he left the house in his PJ's. Fred's eyes were wild but he relaxed a little when they made eye contact with Lisa.

"Oh, sweet angel you're here."

"Fred, are you OK?" It was a dumb question. He was not remotely close to OK, even on a good day, and this was not one of those.

Fred looked around the room and saw the two customers looking at him. He whispered. "No one is OK sweetheart. No one at all."

Lisa waved him towards the counter, getting some distance from the customers.

"Tell me, what is happening Fred?"

Fred took her hand. Lisa almost jumped. She had not expected contact.

"I'm confused, Cyndi. I really am. I thought I knew, but look at this."

Fred opened his notebook to the last page and Lisa read it. As far as she knew she was the only other person to read Fred's notebooks. She always felt a mix of interest and sadness seeing Fred's mental illness laid out on the page.

He watched her reading. "You see, it is me but not me."

She looked up and saw a confusion she didn't normally see. Fred believed what he believed.

"You don't remember writing this?" Lisa let the question hang but he didn't answer. "Because it is your handwriting."

Fred laughed. "Well, it was me, but not me, me. You see?"

Lisa shook her head.

"It is a me from another dimension, an alternate reality. Alternate Fred. You see I thought all this time that the Archons were just evil creatures of pure void; ancient demons before this universe from an existence before time; from a void so cold and cruel that they want nothing more than to bring chaos."

"You don't think that now?"

Fred shook his finger. "They probably still are. I don't know. This other Fred comes from a world where the Archons have freedom. I think he wants to believe we are just two of many Fred's. I think he is not real. A distraction from the agents of the void. But this!" He pointed at the writing. "It is my words!"

Lisa was confused. She was glad it was a slow night. "OK Fred, in English, what is happening?"

"Something is coming out of the hole in the park."

"People's Park?"

"It is a nexus of hate. The Archons are coming from that hole and they are trying to take our world. They're taking the bodies of those whose minds are weak and open. Controlling them like puppets. They detest anything different. They promote hate." He looked up at the menu and back at Lisa. "I'm hungry. Can you get my regular?"

"Yeah Fred," She went to the cooler and grabbed his Coke. "Why haven't they taken my mind? The guys at the park sit by that hole every day, and they seem nice enough."

He opened his Coke can with a snap. "You don't think I listen to the high pitch static for fun, do you? Know, the loud noise you listen to?"

"Punk rock?"

"Yes, whatever. It acts as a vaccination. It blocks the ability of the Archons to control your hate impulses."

Lisa laughed. "Come on, Fred," She opened up the pantry and found that Melissa had already made Fred's daily cheese sandwich. She smiled at the idea of that, unwrapped it and set it on the counter.

"I thought you were different," Fred was bothered and walked away from the counter with his food.

Lisa thought about trying to explain. To talk him out of being angry with her, but what was the point? He was crazy and there was only so much she could do. He ate his sandwich in solitude and, as a song ended, she heard the sounds of sirens. Lots of them.

Lisa ran to the back door and propped it open. When she stepped into the alley, she saw two young boys standing there. There were the ones who had grabbed Fred that day in the park. One of them had a fresh Mohawk and they looked as if they were caught doing something. When they saw her they took off as if they were running from something.

"What are you running from?"

The sirens got louder and closer. The boys probably didn't even hear her yelling. She hadn't heard this many sirens since the last time she was in Chicago. She walked into the intersection of alleys going east-west and north-south. The police cars had all stopped at People's Park, and the air was colored with the red and blue glow of their flashing lights.

Lucas came walking down the alley. He was wiping away the blood from his face.

"What happened?"

He looked back to make sure he wasn't followed. "Big fight. Rednecks everywhere."

She looked towards the park and saw the police with guns raised. "What the hell?"

When she turned back around Lucas had disappeared. She walked back up the steps to the coffee shop when she saw armed cops walking slowly down the alley. She could've sworn they were ten feet tall as their shadows moved unnaturally ahead of them.

Lisa slammed the back door shut. She was seeing things. She turned and Fred stood in the kitchen blocking her path. It made her jump. She was so scared she picked up a hot pad and smacked Fred's arm.

"Fred, you scared the…"

"You saw them, didn't you? Tall as trees with shadows cast not by the sun but the rotten core of the dark universe."

Lisa was breathing heavily. "You're not supposed to be back here."

He left without speaking. Lisa watched as he went all the way out the front door. She wanted to call after him, but she noticed the coffee shop was empty. She suddenly felt more alone than she ever had.

CHAPTER FIFTEEN

It was a bit of a walk for Jonah, Emily, and Justin from downtown to The Savage House. It was located on Second Street, on a corner across from a large parking lot that serviced the hospital.

It looked normal enough. On the west side of the house was a medical supply company, and on the east side were medical offices. It was a big house without any neighbors, which was a good thing because you could hear the music from a block away. The sonic attack escaped every pore of the house. It reminded Justin of an overstuffed suitcase or a sandwich oozing out condiments out the bottom.

When they walked up, the band had just finished a song and seemed to be tuning forever. Random guitar and bass notes were followed by a few seconds of cords and more tuning. Justin took a look across the parking lot to the hospital. The same building where his father died. Last time he walked in those doors he had a father. Just looking at it now made him uncomfortable.

The three of them walked up to the side door. People were lined up outside. Bird, the same guy they saw passing out the flyers, was taking money and stamping hands. Justin was the last to hand over his three dollars. You had to walk through the kitchen and it smelled like an ashtray. The house was full, and everyone was drinking. The floor was slick with spilled beer, and through the tobacco haze Justin saw shapes of people and heard their voices.

"Who do we talk to?" Emily asked.

Before he could answer, the band in the basement erupted. The music exploded and it shook the floor like an earthquake. It was louder than anything

Justin had ever heard. Even louder than his headphones directly over his ear. It felt bone-shaking. Jonah followed the music.

In the corner of the kitchen there was door that looked like a closet. There was a blue light shining within. The three of them followed one another down the shaky wooden planks into the basement. Every inch had a person and they squeezed through until they were on the dirt floor.

An AC unit took up the majority of the space. There was no way that giant machine worked. It felt like it was a thousand degrees in the house.

The room was only slightly bigger than his bedroom, but punks were packed in like sardines. The pop of the fast rhythm cut through as the drummer beat on the snare as if he was clubbing it to death.

Justin stepped back on to the first step of the stairs so he could see the band. The vocals started with a crazy bark. The guy holding the microphone was the same guy who, a short time ago, had punched Kevin Buyers so hard his teeth were left lying in the alley. The Cro-mags shirt was gone. He was standing there with impressive muscles. His many tattoos included a Marine Corps *Semper Fi* and "Detroit Hardcore." As Justin watched him front the band, he instantly understood why he was able to handle himself so well in the fight.

The bass player was a guy he had seen at the park. The guitar player looked like one of the guys that came out of the GTO, but he was shredding. The space was too tight for slam dancing but the crowd as small as it was, tried. A chain of people hit each other until Justin was punched in the gut. He didn't want anyone to see him react, but inside he felt breathless.

Jonah tapped his brother on the shoulder. A group squeezed out past them to leave, creating a spot just big enough for them to move into the basement. Emily was thrilled watching. Justin found himself staring at her for a long moment before she reached up and pulled him into the thick of the crowd. It was chaos in the small pit. Justin never felt anything like it the power of the music; the tribal feeling of the bodies in motion.

Through it all Emily held his hand. He never wanted to let go. In that moment the outside world was gone. He didn't remember why they were there in the first place.

Fred leaned against the Noble Romans pizza restaurant and watched the park from across the street. He held his pocket mirror up and positioned it for a view of the hole at the center of the park. The cops hung around and the red-blue glow lit the area. In his mirror, however, he saw a totally different color; the golden glow of the Archons escaping.

It was as if a geyser spit them into the sky. Invisible to the naked eye, Fred watched as a thousand demons a minute escaped the void.

The door to the pizza place opened and a uniformed worker looked at Fred. "Hey, move on captain pajamas."

Fred turned his mirror to point at the college student and part-time pizza manager. In the mirror, he saw a beast with elephant tusks and a pig nose. The hideous thing was close to threatening violence. "Good evening, sir," Fred bowed. The creature didn't know that he saw his true self. It thought it remained hidden by the veil of the void.

He walked on holding his mirror out to look at the cars in the road. Tanks, dragons, and several monsters wore mounts. The creatures of the void continued to circle and protect the park. Fred stopped when he saw one car driving in the line of monsters. He stared at the blue Chevy Nova that played music as it drove down the road. Fred ran for the first time in years to catch up to the lone car. Luckily it moved slowly, mimicking cruising culture as a cover. Fred looked inside the car. The driver was human although he was wearing aviator sunglasses long after dark.

"Hello?" Fred ran beside the car. "Hello? Sir?"

Fred wanted to know how this man was still human; how they might work together. The man in the car rolled up his window. Fred knocked on it but caught a glimpse of himself in the rearview mirror. The man was laughing in the reflection. There was nothing funny about this moment.

That stopped him. The car moved on. Fred opened his mirror and slowly lifted it up to his face almost afraid to look at his reflection. The face in the mirror had shaved, had more hair and looked calmed and relaxed. That was something he was not feeling.

"Hey there Fred," said the reflection.

Fred turned around to see if anyone was behind him watching. He walked a few more steps until he could lean in front of the bike rack at MacDonald's.

"I know what you are. Another trick of the void to distract me."

Reflection Fred was amused. "Bullshit. If you believed that you would snap this mirror shut. No, no, here we are, Fred. There are no demons. No possession. The hole is a gateway between worlds. You got that much right. They are everywhere in the universe. Black holes, wormholes trans-dimensional gateways. We just happen to live near one. I am sorry it has wrought such havoc on your mind."

Fred smiled. "There is nothing wrong with my mind. This universe is broken, like a crack in the glass of reality that hole is leaking existence. I have seen it. I am the one who is Okey Dokey."

"Really," Reflection tipped his head. "Who is running down the street in his PJ's? I am home with my wife and daughter. You go home to a pile of notebooks and a cat whose owner died six months ago."

"Mrs. Kelly didn't die."

"Her kids just left the cat when they took her earthly belongings to Goodwill. You know her grandson was afraid of you. Do you even know the cat's name?"

Fred took a deep breath. "Ha! You changed the subject. This is not about me."

Reflection nodded. "I disagree. It is about you. You live in a world of abundance and beauty. You waste it on a life detached from a perfectly respectable reality. Do you have any idea what my reality is like?"

"I don't care."

"Oh, Fred Curtis in this reality tied the knot with Catherine. We have a daughter. She is beautiful, likes to hide under the bed. Likes Math, like her parents. Could be a scientist. Except for one problem."

Fred held the mirror at Arm's length. "You expect me to ask."

Reflection Fred grinned. "I'll tell you. This reality is a world dying. Choking on hate, wars that never end. They burned the sky. Slowly we are choking on coal dust. The point is: We are coming for your reality."

"No, no, no. You can't. I won't let you." Fred pointed at the small mirror. "I will fight you with all my energy. I will expose you."

"Too late Fred, one by one, we will take each mind until this reality is devoid and your world is ours."

"I see you, and all the hate mongers at the end of your strings. I will never let you win!"

"Sir, are you okay?"

Fred turned to see a cop. He looked back in the mirror and only his own natural reflection was there.

"Of course, I'm fine." Fred fought to stabilize his breath. "Why wouldn't I be fine?"

The officer didn't say anything. He held a pair of handcuffs. He was clearly an agent of the void. Fred thought he might be licking his lips.

Fred lifted his mirror and saw only the angry cop's face in the reflection. "This is the moment when the void tries to silence me forever," thought Fred. The cop grabbed Fred's arm. The memories from the hospital were hazy, but they flashed before Fred's eyes. He remembered the last time he saw Catherine after he hurt her. He didn't mean to do it. It was an accident, but she didn't trust him after that.

"No, I was just talking," Fred whispered. He couldn't go back to the hospital.

"Officer? Officer!"

Fred looked back to see Zoe, the veteran who also hung out in the park, walking closer.

"Don't waste your time with Fred, officer. He is all right."

Fred looked at the cop. "He doesn't seem all right to me," the cop said.

Zoe approached the cop. "Fred here has been getting the help, I promise you. One vet to another, can you trust me to keep Fred out of trouble?"

"How'd you know I served?" The cop asked.

"I had a feeling." Zoe talked to him about the war. The cop released his grip. Fred slipped away. He kept the mirror in his pocket and just walked home as fast as he could.

Lisa put the espresso on the counter for the woman who had set her books at a window seat while she ran to the bathroom. She was coming up to get it when the front door opened. The bell rang and Lisa looked to see who it was. This time of night it was mostly just regulars. She knew the man. He was the loudmouth veteran who sat drinking in the park all day. His name was Zoe.

Zoe walked to the counter and smiled at Lisa. The smell of whiskey came in the door with him. Despite the smell, he stood straight, not tipsy at all.

"What can I get ya?"

"I don't need a drink darlin'."

Lisa raised an eyebrow. "I suppose you've had enough huh?"

He laughed and leaned on the counter. Lisa felt uncomfortable waiting for him to give a reason for being there.

"Yeah, sorry I don't want to cause no trouble I just wanted to talk to you about Fred."

"What about him?"

"I reckon you are the only person he talks to."

Lisa nodded.

"He almost got himself arrested."

"I tried talking to him." Lisa nervously wiped the counter. "He has new issues I have never heard before. Thinks an alternate reality Fred is trying to influence him."

Zoe nodded. "He sees it in the mirror. I saw him yelling at his mirror; the little one he carries."

Lisa had seen that mirror. She looked at Zoe and was actually charmed that he cared. Fred sat near him in the park almost every day but the two men never talked. It was nice that he was concerned. She laughed inwardly. This proves Fred's theory wrong. Zoe had been in the park day after day, right by the hole with no static or punk rock to inoculate him. Yet, here he was, thoughtfully looking out for the man. Not the actions of an Archon.

"I try my best to help him," she said. "I always ask about how he's feeling."

"That's all I can ask," Zoe smiled and stepped back.

"Hey, I really appreciate you looking out for Fred. Can I get you a drink? On the house."

Zoe shook his head. "That's sweet, but I have to get to the Savage House."

Lisa was taken back. He understood right away what that look meant. He laughed.

"Yeah, I hate that punk bullshit, but they're all my friends, so I go and my ears ring for days." With that, he stepped back outside. Lisa went into the kitchen and over to the sink to start the dishes. She looked up at the mirror above the sink. She turned on the water and soaped the first coffee cup when she glanced at herself in the mirror, she almost dropped the cup. Her reflection wearing goth make-up, like she was going to a show. Her reflection waved.

Lisa did drop the mug this time. When it broke, she looked down at it and then back up to the mirror. Her reflection was back to normal.

She needed to sit down.

Justin stepped outside covered in sweat. Even the humid June air felt chilly after being in the Savage House sweatbox. He saw Jonah talking to his brother, and Zoe the Vet walking up to them, holding a six-pack of Miller Lite with two empty rings.

Emily came out of the basement, equally covered in sweat. She grabbed his hand. Both were damp enough to wrinkle, like they had been in a bath too long. He turned and looked at her green hair in the light glowing out of the kitchen window. She was so beautiful. But only one thing came close to stealing his attention. The hurricane of hardcore that he was in the eye of moments before had captured his mind. Hearing the energy on a record or tape was one thing, but being in the center of the storm was another.

"They think we are crazy," Jonah walked up.

"What?" Justin didn't remember anything before walking into the basement.

"Oh Shit," Emily looked at her watch. "I have to get home."

"No one will help us," Jonah sounded scared.

"I'll walk Emily home. Can you stay with your brother?"

Jonah nodded. Emily and Justin walked away. He should've felt it, but in that moment he felt invincible. He wasn't worried about rednecks, jocks, or body snatchers. He felt ready to take on the world.

CHAPTER SIXTEEN

Fred waited on the corner by the bank and watched the cars – or the image of cars – passing one after the other. During the evening, everything slowed to a crawl as the cruisers slowly drove east and west up and down Kirkwood Ave between the town square and campus. Fred watched the cars.. He didn't need the mirror to know what they really were. He really just needed to find one car.

He heard it before he saw it. Blaring a tune that was cranked so loud the sound stretched the volume well beyond factory standards. It made sense now. Many people listened to loud music, but it took certain pitches and frequencies to block the Archons.

Fred walked closer to the curb and double-checked with his mirror. The car was piloted by a human.

The speakers rattled as the vocalist screamed that he was on a Highway to Hell. Fred found the song foul. He waved at the driver who stopped beside him. The music suddenly faded to nothing, leaving only the rumble of the engine. Fred wanted to say "good evening, sir". He never got the chance.

"Get in," the driver said.

Fred looked around and then pointed to his chest. He had not been inside a car in years. His path was the same every day and he did it all on foot. The thought of being inside a car made his heart race. He felt panic. He looked at the door.

"We ain't got much time fella. so, get in."

Fred reached for the door handle and slid into the comfy leather seat. The AC was on despite all the windows being open. The driver pushed eject on his tape and turned off the radio. He kept up their slow crawl in the direction of the park and campus.

"You're Electric Fred, right?" His drawl felt exhumed from the backest of back waters in southern Indiana. A contrast to Fred's formal-sounding speech.

"Fred Curtis is my name."

The driver laughed. "Shoot. It alight fella', dem kids call me Super-Cruiser. Way, I figure, ain't no need for them or nobody to know my name I ain't here to be remembered for my name. You call me Super-Cruiser, but I'll just call you Fred."

Super-Cruiser kept his hand on the stick shift.

"You know about the Archons, don't you?"

Super-Cruiser nodded. "I just call'em Demons. They come out of that park y'all sit in."

"They might not be demons," Fred said. "I was just talking to an alternate reality version of myself." Fred opened his mirror and held it at an angle so Super-Cruiser could see it. Reflection Fred waved before Fred snapped it shut. "He says they are coming from a dark universe to replace us."

"Hmmm sounds possible. But tell me, Fred, you trust this other you?"

Fred thought about it. There was very little he trusted since the night this all started. He couldn't trust anyone, and now the guy in the mirror was trying to lie to him. First things first he had to know something.

"Who are you really?" Fred asked.

"I'm on your side, Fred." Super-Cruiser laughed. "Would you believe me if I told ya I was a trans-dimensional bounty hunter and this here Nova was gold-lined to prevent nanobot assassins from surfing tachyons into this realm to off me?"

"Sounds possible."

Super-Cruiser laughed. They stopped at a stop sign. A woman crossed in front of the car wearing tight jeans; her hair teased into a corona. Super-Cruiser lowered his sunglasses to get a better look as she passed. Fred saw glowing eyes before he pushed the glasses back up.

"I gotta hand it to your realm buddy, you got all the foxes."

He revved the engine with a rumble as they passed the now empty park.

"Alright, let me level with you, Fred. Ain't nobody gonna believe us, so it ain't worth shit talkin' to no' cops or Chinese Prime Ministers."

Fred felt exposed suddenly. "How do you know about him?"

"Who you think sent my ass here, the Shah of Irune?"

Fred smiled and saluted him. "I knew it."

Super-Cruiser held his finger over his lips to quiet him until they pulled away from the main strip. They went faster. The car thundered without a muffler. They were headed towards Fred's apartment. Super-Cruiser knew exactly where to go.

"Don't believe them, Fred. Don't trust any 'you' besides you. I mean, any other Fred has an agenda. They is trying to stop you from accepting your mission."

Fred smiled as his apartment building came into sight. He would never dismiss the mission.

Justin's ears were still ringing. The echo of the guitar was like the wake of a tide that had left the beach soaked. His head pounded, but it was a good feeling. Long after they walked out of the basement, the music still shook throughout his body.

It took them an hour to make the walk, but Justin didn't feel time pass at all. He had to look at his watch. They were way past anything resembling her curfew. It was the first time Justin had been in the old neighborhood since they moved. It had only been a couple days, but the distance felt daunting when his mom told him they were moving. The only thing that kept him feeling balanced was talking with Emily.

She didn't say much. Justin had nervously talked almost the entire walk home. As they got into the old neighborhood it was as if the ghost of his father was suddenly with him. These were the streets where his father taught him to ride his bike. Emily saw the look on his face.

"What's wrong?"

He didn't want everything to be about his dad. Everywhere he went he saw him. He wondered when it would end, or if it would end. He felt like he couldn't talk to her about it. Justin shook his head. They walked the last couple blocks in silence. Justin felt a bit of an impossible chill on the warm summer evening. The sky clouded up.

Emily looked at her watch. "My dad is going to kill me."

Justin nodded. By the time he skateboarded back across town, his mom was going to be furious, too. She probably was an hour ago. They stopped in front of the McRoberts' house. The lights inside were red. The color of the house looked odd to him, too. Justin felt weird about this.

"Are you sure?"

"Where else can I go? It's my home."

He knew she was right. She squeezed his hand and pulled him in for a kiss. He dropped his deck and held her. Their lips mingled. His heart stopped as she pulled away.

"I don't know when I'll be able to see you again."

"I'll wait," It was a stupid thing to say. He tried to save the embarrassment. "I mean, I will stay here a few minutes to make sure you're safe."

She gave him a quicker but more intense kiss. He could still taste her sweat as she opened the front door. Weak-kneed, Justin fell back into the grass. He needed a minute anyways. It was weird, he knew it, but he smelled her hair on his hand, so he sat there behind the bushes smelling his fingers.

The lights came on in the house. The yelling started right away. He only made out bits and pieces through the walls. Where was she? Who was she with? What had she done to her hair? Justin had only seen his neighbor, Joe

McRoberts, playing ball with his kids, or walking to his enormous grill. He had never heard him yell like that.

It was hard to listen to, but he expected it. He thought they were calming down. He considered walking away. What could he really do? The voices got quieter. Justin picked up his skateboard and was seconds from rolling away when he heard Emily scream. It wasn't anger. It wasn't defiance. She was screaming bloody murder.

"Juuuuuuuustin! Heeeeeellllllp!"

Justin ran at the house holding the skateboard by the bottom trucks. He reached for the door handle and swung the door open. Joe McRoberts and his oldest son John held Emily down by her arms. Tammy McRoberts had scissors and a chunk of green hair in her hands.

"Get off her!" Justin screamed.

Joe McRoberts dropped his daughter's arm and grabbed a butcher knife off the counter. Justin ran at him using the skateboard like he was Captain America. He hit the man knocking them both back. He held the father down with the deck and heard screams around him. When he looked up a knife went straight into Joe's head. His body twitched and Justin fell back.

"What the fuck?" Justin yelled and squirmed across the floor to get back before the blood pooled under Joe's body. Justin looked up to see John McRoberts collapsing; a knife was in his forehead. He thumped to the floor. Justin looked up to see Emily slamming a knife into her mother's chest. She reached to the counter and grabbed the last of the large knives in the butcher block.

"Woah Emily, Woah." Justin was afraid to stand up.

Emily stood over her mother who shook her butchered hair at her.

"What are you?" Emily screamed.

Her mother spit up blood pinned to the floor. She tried to reach for her. She gargled blood as she spoke. "Conform...conform...accept the intolerance of the world to come."

Emily looked at Justin, her eyes overtaken by fear. He was too stunned to react.

Her father Joe McRoberts' dead body began to glow. Then her brother lit up like the ass-end of a lightning bug. They burned so bright Justin had to close his eyes. When he opened them, the bodies had disappeared. Only the knives remained on the floor. He looked up at Emily. "What happened?"

"They were going to kill me."

Her Mom finally stopped struggling. Her body was only lifeless for a few seconds before her skin began to glow. Justin watched this time through squinting eyes. Her body disappeared into the light. The little flame flickered before rising to the ceiling. Three tiny flames hovered in the air above them.

Emily looked up at the flames floating near the ceiling. "That's them. Whatever they are?"

Justin wanted to call the police, but not only had his new girlfriend stabbed her family, he knew they couldn't possibly trust anyone to understand why. How could they explain this?

"What did you do with my family???"

Emily fell into Justin's arms and cried. He knew where he could hide her. He grabbed her hand and picked up his skateboard. "Come on. Grab your bike."

CHAPTER SEVENTEEN

Lisa watched the clock on the wall at the Spoon tick slowly toward 11 p.m. when she could close. She had all the dishes done, she had wiped all the empty tables and Mark, the editor of the student radical journal, was the only customer left. He was at that same table most nights when it was time to close. Finally, the clock ticked over to closing time.

"Mark," She didn't have to say more. He said nothing. Just picked up his stuff and silently handed her his coffee cup. She smiled and walked back into the kitchen. She jumped when she saw a shape in the small space. It was a person hidden by shadow. Lisa flicked on the light and relaxed when she saw the co-owner of the restaurant. Her name was Ursula. At least that was the name she asked to go by. You never know with hippies.

"Jesus, Ursula you scared the shit out of me."

The middle-aged hippie woman stood silently in the kitchen wearing a sundress. Lisa waited for her to apologize but she said nothing. Lisa was confused. She had dead-bolted the back door and she didn't think Ursula could've come in without her noticing. She glanced back at the door. She didn't remember it opening.

"I was just locking up," Lisa said. "One more dish to do." She went over to the sink. Still, her boss said nothing. She soaped the cup, feeling the eyes locked on her back.

Ursula finally spoke. "What was that music you were playing?"

Lisa put the cup in the drying rack. She hadn't played any music in a while. "I just play the tapes Bob leaves in the deck." It was a lie, but they were only supposed to play approved music. Lisa looked over and felt relief knowing that she had cleared her tape, and put Bob's tape back in. She pointed at the tape deck. "Smooth Jazz, all night."

Ursula squinted and Lisa felt judged. "All night?"

Lisa nervously laughed. "Yep, all night."

"You think this funny?" Ursula sounded like a scolding parent.

Lisa shook her head and started switching off the lights, leaving only the kitchen light on. "I don't have time for this. I have to study, and it is already late."

Lisa got out her keys and started to walk out. She was almost to the door when she thought she heard the word "freak." It was spoken with a venom she didn't know her old hippie boss was capable of. She was turning around to say "excuse me", when she noticed the Kitchen was empty and dark. Lisa exhaled and almost fell over. She ran back into the kitchen. No one was there.

"Ursula?" Her voice echoed in the empty shop.

She turned back to the mirror over the sink. She saw her reflection in the mirror. Nothing looked out of place, but she ran to get outside as fast as she could. Everything felt wrong. She couldn't get out fast enough.

Out of the air conditioning into the warm summer heat, Lisa took deep breaths as she walked.

"You're not crazy," she told herself several times, but doubt crept in.

It was impossible for her not to think about Fred. All the crazy theories he had told her over the year she worked at the Spoon. All the ways she dismissed him. He said the demons were replacing the people. She had never seen Ursula act that way.

Lisa gripped both straps of her backpack as she walked up Kirkwood towards the park. The street was busy with cruisers. The muscle cars were out in force; a few polluted the air with music ranging from Boston to ZZ Top. She stopped when she got to the wall. The park was empty. Everyone was at the Savage House show. Her eyes scanned until she found the gaping wound in the middle of the park. It was taped off.

A car on the far side of the road drove slowly by playing "Sharp Dressed Man." The guy in the passenger seat climbed up so he sat in the window with his arms on the hood. "Hey, Bride of Frankenstein," the driver shouted. "When's the funeral?"

Lisa was not even dressed that goth, just fishnet stockings, and combat boots. She kept walking. Sadly, the dorm was in the direction the car was moving. ZZ Top got turned down.

"Hey Morticia," He laughed and his buddies in the car thought it was hilarious. Being a goth kid on the southside of Indianapolis, she had heard all these jokes before. Shouted in the halls of Southport high school, or out of the window of monster trucks in the parking lot. These redneck shitheads were so base they had no idea that they made the exact same insults over and over. As if the Skaters never heard "skate or die" a thousand times, or punks with mohawks never heard the Tonto jokes.

She kept walking and they followed. She passed the bike shop and looked in the window for an instant. The glow from the Von Lee movie theater and the light reflected in the glass stopped her. She saw herself but it was like she stood in front of a painting of Dante's nightmare. In the reflection, there were no cars, only demons massing like a storm on the horizon.

She turned and saw the redneck stepping into the street from a car. He was drunk. "Come here you fuckin' whore, I want to know if you taste like a normal girl."

Lisa was aware of how alone she was. She took off running as fast as she could. If Spaceport was open, she would have gone there. There was no one in the ticket office of the movie theater. There was a payphone, but what would the police do? They wouldn't believe her and worse they would probably make fun of her too. She had to get home. She ran until her legs burned and by the time she entered campus they had turned around.

Nicolette Morgan was not mad when her son came in after curfew. Justin came in through the basement and found her sitting in front of the TV. The lights were out. The cable box glowed, and she had on the shopping network. Her face was only lit by the glow of the TV, but her eyes were wide and unblinking.

"Mom?"

She didn't respond. Her attention was on the saleswoman on the TV who was selling a handbag.

"Trust me when I say you'll be the talk of the neighborhood if you buy this handbag. It is perfect for every situation and, most importantly, you won't stand out."

"I need one. I don't want to stand out," his mom whispered.

Justin walked to the TV and turned the dial so it clicked off.

"Why did you do that?" She looked at him. Justin fought back tears. He had already lost his father and he was desperate to believe this was still his mother. Part of him wanted to run to her and hug her. He was scared and needed her to hold him.

His mom's eyes looked different. His mother was not in there and he was afraid to get close. At the same time, she looked weak and tired. Maybe these demons used lots of energy.

"Go to bed mom," He had an agenda of course. She nodded and disappeared up the stairs. He followed behind and made sure the bedroom door closed. Then he went to the side door and turned the deadbolt slowly so it wouldn't snap. He opened the door let Emily in. When he shut the door, he put his finger over his lips.

He took Emily by the hand and slowly walked her to the basement. His mom had set up a little guest room next to her office in the basement. He grabbed a bath towel from the basement bathroom. When they got to the tiny room without windows, he looked at her. It was the first time he had seen her with her butchered hair. He still thought she was beautiful.

"If you turn on a light put the towel under the door," he said.

"Justin, I can't thank you enough."

He waved her off. He wanted to stay and hold her and make her feel better, but he knew he should give her space. "You're safe down here till morning. I promise."

Emily gave a pat on the bed. "I don't want to be alone."

Every molecule in Justin's body freaked out. She wasn't saying what he thought she was saying.

She smiled. "Just stay. We both need sleep, but I can't be alone."

Just sleep she said. He kicked off his shoes. He slid onto the bed, over the cover. She put her arms around him. She was asleep almost immediately, breathing deeply. He left the light on; afraid he might see the glowing creatures her family transformed into if the room went dark. The first time he closed his eyes he saw her dad with a knife in his head and turning into a ghostly flame. His eyes shot open, and he lay there listening to Emily's soft breathing. Eventually, he slept.

CHAPTER EIGHTEEN

Fred slowly opened his eyes. It was morning.

After the Supercruiser dropped him off, he only had the energy to put his notebook in the drawer and fall on the bed. He still had on his Chuck Taylors and his pajama suit.

He sat up and looked out the window. He had been too nervous to look earlier, but he wasn't even sure what he was afraid to see. It was possible he had slept through the entire Archon invasion and the nuclear fallout was raining ash outside his window.

Everything looked normal. He didn't know how long he slept. The sun was out. The morning was already warming up. He heard his neighbor's window air conditioning unit turn on. He looked for his watch. It was gone leaving only a tan line. The neighbor's cat was at the end of the bed, stretched out. She looked at him with a curious expression.

Suddenly he felt a dagger in his mind. The cat finally spoke. "What are you waiting for?" The cat then bound off the bed toward the bathroom. Fred chased her "I'll read it when I am good and ready."

Fred turned to his nightstand. The cat had to be talking about the notebook. The drawer was slightly opened. He knew he had pushed it tight. This time the cat stood on the back of the toilet tank. "No time to waste, Freddy."

Fred chased the cat again. She expertly jumped through the hole in the window screen that had been her door for months. Fred shut the window. "Oh no, this arrangement will not work. Only my Goddamn mother called me Freddy."

He opened the drawer. It was empty. No notebook. Fred gasped. He knew he put it in there last night. Fred ran back to the kitchen where his backpack hung on its hook. He rifled through it even though he knew he had put it in the drawer before he went to sleep.

FUCK! Fred picked up a coffee mug and threw it at the sink. It stopped short of the sink in mid-air. Fred stared at it. It was as if a string held it. Fred karate chopped the air above it, and below. It still floated in the air.

"Shit," Fred cursed and suddenly the mug shot like a missile into the bathroom. He heard the cup smash into pieces. Fred ran after it and stopped when he looked in the mirror. A small piece of the mug must have hit it. Three jagged cracks went down the center of the mirror.

On the edge, he saw himself. In his pajamas, balding, what hair he had was going wild. In the center, he saw himself in a tweed jacket, finely groomed; the Fred who he had spoken to earlier. In the third section of the mirror, his reflection wore a leather jacket and mirror shades.

"No!" Fred pointed his finger. "No, no absolutely no way."

Professor Fred in the middle rolled his eyes. High-Tech Fred laughed.

"We have to talk," the two reflected Freds said together.

"Yeah, professor in the middle. Where is my notebook? It is *my* notebook."

Justin made his way upstairs early. He walked around the house looking for his mother. He slowly opened her bedroom door, but she wasn't there. He noticed a burn mark on the ceiling above the bed. When he touched the covers, they were wet and warm.

"Moooom?" He walked through the house. He felt a little panic. When he got to the kitchen he stopped and looked out the back door. Ray was asleep in a lawn chair on the deck, his bike beside him.

He opened the back door. "Dude, what happened?"

He shook his head "For starters, my brother turned into a spider-minotaur thing and chased me. My parents got taken over dude. It's like that stupid movie."

"Invaders from Mars," Justin nodded. He put up a finger. "Come inside. My mom is gone."

"Fuck dude, she is probably helping my parents build a flying saucer."

Emily came out of the basement. She must have had clothes in her backpack. She had changed into a different shirt.

"Woah, uh hey Emily."

"They got my parents too," Emily sat at the kitchen table.

Justin got them all cereal and caught Ray up on what happened. He wasn't shocked. Even when he explained that Emily killed her family and watched them turn into beings of light.

"You realize what this means right?" Ray took a deep breath. Justin didn't know what to say so he just waited for him to continue. "The guy in the park, the crazy one?"

"Electric Fred," added Emily.

"Not so crazy now, is he?" Ray asked.

"We should go talk to him." Justin went to the phone and dialed. "We gotta talk to Jonah, too, make sure he is safe."

"Have him meet us at the park," Emily put her bowl in the sink.

Ray nodded. Justin put his hand on his shoulder. "We'll figure it all out, dude."

The phone kept ringing. Justin nervously waited until the answering machine came on and the beep, then he said, "Jonah, this Ray. Justin and Emily and I are just checking to make sure you are okay. Meet us at the...you know where." He hung up.

Justin hoped if Jonah's body-snatched mom listened to the machine she wouldn't know where they were meeting, but Ray would. Ray passed him his skateboard and they went out the side door.

Lisa walked into the park after hardly sleeping. She didn't feel like she had even closed her eyes the entire night. Sleep was troubling. When she closed her eyes, she saw all the unexplainable things. She thought about Fred all night. She had reached an inescapable conclusion: He was correct. Or she was also crazy. But, if they both saw the same things, then it had to mean they were not crazy. Right?

She waited until ten, knowing that was normally the time-of-day Fred first made his way to the park. When she turned the corner, she found the park almost empty. Zoe sat at the back in his normal spot. When she got closer, she could tell he was hungover. His eyes were bloodshot, and his breathing was as labored as a broken iron lung. He wheezed in pain.

Lisa sat next to him as he cracked open a 40 Oz. beer in a bag. "Mornin'"

"You seen Fred since we talked?"

Zoe seemed confused. "We talked? I don't remember that."

Lisa sighed.

"I'm sorry sweetheart," he said. "You know how many rice paddies I walked through during my year in shit, my feet soaked in more agent orange than I care to think about? Could be the drink or Monsanto but I don't remember us talking."

She nodded and felt a little defeated. At that point, two kids on skateboards and one on a BMX bike came into the park. It took Lisa a moment, but she was pretty sure one of them was in the alley the night before. Lisa didn't recognize the girl.

"You folks see Electric Fred?"

Lisa felt protective. "What do you want with Fred?"

"Why does everybody want to see Fred all the sudden?" Zoe laughed. "Who are you anyway?"

The oldest boy introduced himself and his friends. Justin did the talking. "Everything he told us is coming true." Lisa listened as he told them about their experiences, and it sounded like hers. All the nasty behavior, the odd reflections, and the angry rednecks. She told them what she saw as Zoe finished his beer. He dropped the can and crushed it under his foot.

Lisa turned to look at him.

"Oh, y'all think Fred is some kind prophet now huh? Let tell you about Fred. I've known Fred since the *Vets Against the War* days. Yeah, they liked having one of us vets around."

"Fred was a protestor?" Lisa was shocked.

"Protestor, shit he was an honor roll astronomy student. knew everything about galaxies and shit. He and his girlfriend were at all the rallies."

"Girlfriend?" Lisa was still shocked.

"I think he was close to marrying her. they were at all the rallies. Fred was a justice-minded guy before the incident."

Zoe let that hang out there. They were all interested in what he had to say.

"You want to know what made Fred? It was what made this park, really. You see this park didn't exist in the Sixties. There was a store here owned by some hippie dude that lived on some commune he was trying to build south of town in Bean Blossom. He rented the storefront out to students from the Black Panther party."

"What's that?" Ray asked.

"Black radicals, they were big on the west coast."

"Yep," Zoe nodded. "Being that IU was only desegregated not too long ago, it was a big deal when these black folk opened their store and called it the Black Market. Now this town ain't so bad, but as a black man let tell you, serving didn't stop nobody around here from calling me, n*****. And they didn't like no Black Market."

"Something bad happened," Justin whispered.

"I don't know what Fred was doing there after midnight, but one night after Christmas he saw the Klan tossing firebombs. Shit, can you imagine wasting perfectly good vodka to burn down the store?"

Lisa looked around at the park. She never knew the history and felt ashamed that she had sat so many hours here and never knew the history of it.

"The Hippies were copying off Berkley. They had a sit-in and demanded the land become a park where they could teach positive change. Old Fred Curtis, he never bought that. He thought the ground was tainted. Cursed or evil. That is why he sits here every day."

Lisa heard enough. She got up and walked in the direction where she knew Fred lived. She wasn't sure which apartment, but she knew the building. The kids were following her.

"You're going to talk to Fred, aren't you?"

"Bet your ass I am."

CHAPTER NINETEEN

Professor Fred smiled. "Yeah, about that notebook. There are a lot of damning things in there."

Fred shook his head. "You can't have it. Give it back."

"He already has it," said High-Tech Fred.

"We can't have your reality using reflections to expose us. I'm sorry Fred, but we are coming. There is nothing you can do to stop us. You might as well heal those ears and let me have that body."

Fred pointed his finger at the mirror. "No, no I know the truth. I can stop you."

"You don't know shit," High-Tech Fred pointed at the center reflection. "He is nothing. No threat to you or anyone."

"You have seen what we can do Fred. We took the bodies of parents, of cops, we control authority figures, and we unleashed the conformist hate. You saw it in the reflections."

"I did, and I have for years. Before the hole in the park was opened up and sped everything up." Fred walked back to a pile of notebooks from 1984 and picked up the one on top. "Right here. Five years ago I wrote about the hateful energy under the land in People's Park. I sat there every day trying to block it, to expose it. I should get a goddamn purple fucking heart for the hours I sat listening to Zoe, to the kids with the funny hair and spiked collars. I saw it all."

"I know you did Fred," High-Tech Fred said. "Well, you think you saw it all, and I know it all feels very real. The programmers are masters at illusion."

"Programmers?" Fred looked at an older pile of notebooks. For a second it felt like the floor dropped out from under him. He looked at the notebooks from the seventies. Fred shook his head. "No, I proved that wrong in 1977."

"Proved what wrong?" Professor Fred was curious.

"Tell him, Fred." High-Tech Fred spoke softly "Tell him what happened in March of 1974."

"It wasn't God," Fred spoke with anger.

High-Tech Fred nodded. "Close enough."

"Don't listen to him," Professor Fred pointed at the reflection of High-Tech Fred. "He is a liar!"

"No," High-tech Fred cracked his knuckles. "I am the truth. Fred, you know none of this is real."

"It is real, Fred understands physics. There are multiple universes at play here. My universe is no less real."

"Stop," High-Tech laughed. "You're confusing him for no reason. Fred, you saw it yourself in 1974. This reality is too perfect. The chances that a sun and planet would dance at just the perfect distance for billions of years, long enough to evolve a species that could survive and develop without a space rock creaming them into putty. No, much too insane."

"What is he saying, Fred?" Professor Fred was angry.

"No, this is not a simulation!" Fred almost spit with anger.

Professor Fred rolled his eyes. High-tech Fred laughed. "Every supernova and every blink, programmed to test your mind. Every tangible motion is a code written into the machine that thinks it is Fred Curtis the Earthling."

"Bullshit!" Fred made a fist and punched the mirror. It shattered. Fred felt the cuts on his fist and held his hand. His hand hurt but he forgot about it when he looked down. There were many hundreds of pieces reflecting up. Some were tiny but a dozen or so were big enough for Fred to see various versions of himself: long-haired Fred, shaved head Fred, baseball player Fred, naked Fred, bandana Fred, trenchcoat Fred, white suit and pink shirt Fred. He heard a chorus of voices. They called his name. A few screamed. All Fred could do was slam the bathroom door shut and bury his face in his pillow.

Fred cried long enough to need a tissue. When he sat up, he was looking straight into his nightstand mirror. Professor Fred watched him.

"You want to believe him you can, but I command the agents of the void, Fred. I know you and your minions are on to us."

"Minions? I don't have minions."

"You want a war, Fred? This is a war of the worlds! I shall crush any who oppose us."

Jonah rolled over in bed. He didn't remember going to sleep. His boots and skateboard were on the floor by the door that stayed open all night. He looked at his record player and there was an LP from the band NOMEANSNO where he left it days before. He switched on the stereo, and turned the tab to "record player." He thought back to the first time he ever played a *Bad Brains* record. He had listened to three songs at 45 RPMs when the record was supposed to be played on 33.

His brother heard the ultra-fast, almost Mickey Mouse-sounding version of "The Big Takeover" coming out of the speakers and came into his room to make fun of him. When the song finished, he dropped the needle on the current record and walked to the bathroom in the hallway.

The house was empty. His brother never came home from the show, but he was a freshman at IU and didn't have a curfew like Jonah did. He had expected a mouthful from his mother when he came in after midnight. Instead, he found the TV tuned to the home shopping network., The cable converter box was warm enough to tell him that it had been on for hours. His mom, however, was no longer in the living room.

He still had not seen her this morning. "Mom?" He walked to her bedroom door and knocked twice. It wasn't that weird for her not to notice. She had been detached ever since Jonah's father got re-married two years ago. She had never been an overbearing mother, to begin with. Since that time, they could get away with lots of things, as long as their grades stayed up.

His mother wanted to be a hip parent. She constantly tried to play sides and always pointed out that their father was more than happy to move to Pittsburgh, of all places. They had fun visiting him there, but she made it sound like it was a hellhole devoid of culture.

Jonah pushed her bedroom door open. "Hey Ma, you better be dressed. I'm coming in." The room was empty. It wasn't normal for her to leave without a note. After his weird experience at the record store and all the stories going around, he supposed it was better that she wasn't home.

He had to piss and went into his mother's bathroom. He needed a shower. He was covered in sweat from the basement show. His hair was a sticky mess. He needed more than a pee.

He had his hand on the switch when he realized the room was already faintly lit. It looked like a Mothra-sized lighting bug had floated into the bathroom, up by the ceiling in the corner. It kept hovering, Jonah wondered what it was until he looked in the giant mirror. In the reflection he saw a ghostly version of his mother. His jaw dropped.

"Don't be scared Jonah dear. It's your mother." The voice was distorted. It floated in the air like an echo.

Jonah took a step back. "The fuck you are."

The ghost in the mirror smiled, and it looked like her. "I am your mother from the other side of the void. Your father and I need you."

She and his father couldn't talk. Not unless it was through the lawyers. He rolled his eyes.

"We can be a family again, never apart," she said.

He couldn't wait to pee. He turned around and walked toward his bathroom. The floating light followed him. Jonah turned and slammed the door.

"Jonah, please." It sounded like his mother and this time it sounded as if she was in the room.

"Leave me alone!"

Jonah barely made it to the toilet which he shared with his brother. The seat was up as always. He let out a sigh as he finally released. Afterwards, he went to the sink to wash his hands and almost missed it. Their medicine cabinet was small. He wasn't looking up. His reflection was more dressed than he was. He looked like an extra in *The Road Warrior*; his hair was cut into a red mohawk, and he was wearing black shoulder pads with spikes on it.

"What the fuck?" Jonah stepped back. "Pretty good look."

Jonah laughed. His reflection did not. "We need you, Jonah."

"For what?"

"Your friends are trying to stand in the way of progress. They are trying to stop the new world."

Jonah reached up and touched the mirror. It turned to liquid at his touch. On the other side, the warrior Jonah reached up. The coarse warrior hand met his and Jonah felt a surge of power.

"I thought you wanted to spread hate, conformity," Jonah said.

"Don't worry about that. Think about our family," Warrior Jonah said.

"What do you mean?"

Warrior Jonah smiled. "Dad never left, and when we come to your world, we will be together."

"What does removing all the punk records at the store have to do with this?"

Warrior Jonah blinked out of view for just a second. Jonah thought he saw Electric Fred.

"Music is a small price to pay to have our family. Pledge yourself to the new world."

CHAPTER TWENTY

Justin nervously tapped on his skateboard as Lisa looked through the notebook. A few months back Fred gave her a notebook that was mostly drawings. It was the first time he called her an angel. She knew he had written his address in it at some point.

Justin and Ray nervously fidgeted. The complex was northwest of downtown in a neighborhood none of them had ever been in. It wasn't ghetto but it was shabbier than anything they were normally around. This neighborhood was government housing. Ray had heard kids mocked at school for living at the hill. He never heard of it before middle school.

"This is the hill huh," Ray said softly.

"Yeah, the grit pit," Justin said, using the other unkind name the kids called it.

"No one should be made fun of for not having money," Lisa said as she thumbed through the notebook.

"Yeah, not cool," Emily added.

Justin felt misunderstood. He never got the chance to explain himself. Lisa found the address. She pointed to the apartment. They walked over and Lisa didn't waste time. She knocked. Emily, Justin, and Ray lined up their decks and bike in the courtyard outside Fred's door. They had a long ride to get here. Lisa had a ten-speed, Emily and Justin had to work hard on the skateboards to keep pace.

Another knock, "Fred open up. It's Lisa from the Spoon."

Justin looked across the courtyard as a feral looking cat walked towards them.

"He must not be home," said Emily.

"No, we would've seen him walking to the park." Lisa tried the handle. It was locked.

The cat rubbed up against Justin's leg. "He's home."

They all turned and looked at Justin and then down his leg. The gray striped cat looked up at them with the natural cat judgment.

"Did the cat say that?" Ray asked.

The cat nodded.

"Why is the cat talking?" Emily asked.

Lisa shrugged.

They were all staring at the cat as she went under a bush and used her nose to nudge a rock over. Justin smiled when he saw the hidden house key. He grabbed the key and handed it to Lisa. No one was surprised when it fit right in the lock. Lisa slowly opened the door. Justin was right behind her.

"Fred, its Lisa. I'm here with friends. We just need to talk."

The door opened and the smell hit them first. Justin wasn't sure this apartment had been cleaned in years. Inside the space was filled with piles of notebooks, newspapers, and magazines. Fred was nowhere to be seen.

The kitchen had no dishes except coffee cups. Even the kitchen table was covered in more piles of notebooks. The walls had articles from science magazines and journals that were stapled to the wall. There were enough to look like wallpaper and went from floor to ceiling. Most of them were old and yellowing against the wall.

Justin scanned the titles. They all had various headlines about multiple universes, time being an illusion and various conspiracy theories, with just a hint of science. Justin stopped at a picture of Einstein. Someone had written on it in magic-marker: "In what universe did he prove his theory?"

"Fred?" Lisa called out before she pushed open the bedroom door. Justin looked over her shoulder just as she gasped. Fred was on his bed holding a large knife. He was crying, his face red. His body shook. The knife danced at the end of his arm.

"Get out of here!" Fred sobbed. "I thought you were an angel, but you're just another agent of the void."

"Show him your reflection!" Justin suggested. Lisa ran to his mirror so he could see her face. He relaxed. In a matter of seconds, he went back to crying again.

"We can't stop him! The Archons have already taken so many. We can't find them all. I was getting up the courage...if we can't stop them, we have to hide. If we can't hide, we may have to kill ourselves before they turn us into agents of the void."

"Slow down Fred. Slow down," Lisa said.

Fred was suddenly angered and his whole mood changed. "Oh, I see. You are going to tell me I'm crazy just like the others. The other Fred, he wants to confuse me, trick me into giving up. It almost worked, it almost worked."

"No Fred," Lisa rubbed his shoulder.

"Stop it! You want to put me back in the hospital with all the looney tunes whackos. Go ahead, ignore the big fat stinking truth right under your nose."

He sobbed. Lisa was crying with him. She pulled him into a hug. She whispered over his shoulder. "We believe you, Fred, we've seen them. We need your help to stop them."

Justin watched Fred's wet eyes lock onto him. "And who are you? My own personal Fellowship of the Ring?"

"I guess we are," Justin knew what he meant because he had read all three Lord of the Rings books with his father.

Lisa still had her hand on Fred's shoulder. "OK tell us everything. Start with the bombing of the park..."

Fred squinted at Lisa. He was shocked. It was clear on his face. "How'd you know about that?"

"It's history. We read about it at the library before we came over."

Fred took a deep breath. "It was a hateful act. It cut like a burning hot dagger into this community, but sadly not everyone was upset. There is something about the anger and hatred that tears little holes between universes. I can't explain the science," he said. "In their world, they are fighting for survival. They figured out some way to turn themselves into beings of pure energy. That is how they take their bodies. They come out of the hole looking for a host."

Justin looked back at Emily and Ray. "See, it is not them anymore."

"Can we get our parents back?" Ray asked.

Fred hesitated. He looked away. "I'm sorry. I think they're gone."

"Let's just fill in the hole," said Emily.

"It needs to be sealed in concrete, or they will seep through the soil."

Ray raised his hand. "I can make concrete; I helped make our basketball court. But I gotta know something."

"Anything," Fred smiled. He seemed proud to be taken seriously.

"Why the fuck does your cat talk?"

Fred looked confused, but before he could answer, the window exploded. Justin turned to see Jonah in the apartment doorway. He had muscles they had never seen before, no shirt, black spiked shoulder pads, and a freshly-cut, red-dyed mohawk. He looked different but there was no mistaking his face.

"Jonah!"

Justin wondered why his friend had an ax in his hand.

"Dude, we tried calling you," Justin smiled until the ax was lifted into the air. Lisa was shocked by the sight of a cartoonishly big and evil-looking version of the kid she saw in the alley the night before. Lisa pushed Fred down before the ax flew through the air and stuck in the wall. Lisa held Fred down and looked up. Justin and Ray leapt toward their friend. Emily was helping Lisa to lift Fred. It took all Lisa's strength.

"Get him out of here," Justin yelled as he traded awkward blows with his friend. Justin hit the floor, but Ray, who fought with his brother his whole life, was less phased.

Lisa pulled on Fred who insisted on getting his backpack. "Wait!" Fred yelled as he grabbed one of the empty notebooks. Lisa and Emily focused on getting Fred out the door as the guys wrestled with Jonah.

"I am the new world order, an agent of the void!" Jonah screamed as he attacked his friends relentlessly. Lisa could hear the whacks they were taking from the next room. Fred continued to grab clothes, his pen, whatever he could reach.

"You said the punk music protected our minds, what happened to him?"

"I don't know!" Fred screamed.

Ray took two vicious hits as he tackled Jonah. They both stood on wobbly feet as Justin pushed Jonah into Fred's bathroom. Ray and Justin held the door shut.

"I am the agent of the void," Jonah yelled before dozens of voices joined him yelling in anger from behind the door.

"Who else is in there?" Lisa asked.

Justin and Ray struggled to hold the door shut, but Jonah was close to pushing it open.

"Go! Get him out of here!" Justin yelled. Emily grabbed a chair from the kitchen table, dumping notebooks onto the floor in the process. She placed the chair under the door handle. They all looked at one another, impressed at her solution.

They left the house together, walking outside into the afternoon sun.

It was hot, Lisa felt delirious, and worse, it was like every car that passed seemed to be watching them.

CHAPTER TWENTY-ONE

Justin unlocked the side door and let his friends into the house. Ray and Emily both went to the fridge to get sodas. Lisa helped Fred who was muttering under his breath for the whole walk. She tried talking to him, but Fred was not interested in the conversation. He seemed to be working something out on his own.

It was almost dinner time. Justin didn't look for his mother. He was sure the creature from the other dimension had already taken his mother and possibly destroyed her. He only recently moved here, but the house felt empty without his mother.

"We don't know that our parents are really gone," said Emily.

Fred stopped. He turned to face them. "I'm sorry my dear, but there is little reason for hope."

"Hey, I want Fred to get some rest," Lisa said as she guided him by the shoulder, out of the room.

Justin led the way into the basement and opened the guest bedroom for Fred. Lisa held his arm until they got into the windowless room. He slipped off his shoes and sat on the bed. He snapped his fingers at his backpack. "I need my notebook, my dear."

Lisa handed him a pen and the notebook. "Fred, if you understand what's going on, you have to help us."

Fred smiled. "It is not a simulation," Fred looked at Justin. "Stay put, I will find answers."

"I think you should sleep," Lisa said.

"My mind is stronger than anyone realized. Is it possible that we are all correct, all the Fred's in the rainbow?" He giggled. Lisa smiled as she stepped out and closed the door.

Justin felt a little nervous around this older beautiful woman. "Why doesn't he get help?"

Lisa shrugged. "Lots of people care about Fred. Don't forget, he was right. Being able to see through the lies; is there a better reason for losing your mind?"

Justin looked at the door and nodded.

She pointed at his chest. "Don't let Fred leave. You understand?"

Emily and Ray were at the top of the stairs and they didn't hide their fear. Justin knew how they felt. Lisa was only twenty years-old but she was the only adult they had to lean on.

"I'll be right back," Lisa said.

"Where you going?" Ray fumbled on his words. "You can't just leave us."

"Just lock the doors, don't open them for anyone. I just need to get us some help. Someone else has to have seen all this."

"We can handle ourselves," Ray insisted.

Lisa went out the front door. They just watched her go. Ray nervously asked the obvious question, "We're going to haul concrete down to the park on our skateboards?" Justin locked the door behind her. Ray and Emily stood there staring at him. He wasn't sure how he earned leadership position, but they were looking to him for what to do next.

"Come on. I'll throw a tombstone pizza in the oven," While Justin was making their dinner, Ray looked out the window. The night was coming. The hue of summer dusk was darkening the sky outside. The horror of it all crawled into Justin's mind as he tried to focus on just making them food.

"This is like the movie a couple weeks ago on Sammy Terry," said Ray.

"What movie?" asked Emily.

"It was called *Phantasm*. The monsters came from another dimension."

Justin looked out the window. He knew the movie. He had hours of the local horror host introducing horror movies sitting downstairs on a VHS.

Justin ran down the stairs to the new TV and searched through the tapes until he found it. In his handwriting in sharpie it said Phantasm/Ten Diagram Pole Fighter. It was one of his dozen or more Sammy Terry/Black belt theater double features.

He waited as the tape rewound it so he could watch it again. He stopped near the beginning and watched Sammy climb out of the coffin. George the little plastic toy spider lowered on the string so Sammy could talk to it. Emily and Ray came in behind him and they watched together.

"Good evening, I am your host, Sammy Terry, tonight George a truly ghoulish mind Phantasm while teach you a valuable lesson..."

Justin pointed at the screen. "Here it is, Listen."

"There is nothing more horrifying than the terrors in our own mind."

"What are you trying to say?

Justin looked pained, in fear. "What if we can't escape, because it is in here. He pointed at his head.

Emily stood up and hugged Justin. He closed his eyes for a moment and enjoyed the feeling of her arms around him. "We'll face it together." She didn't sound afraid. It was exactly what he needed to hear. She had been everything he needed, right when he needed it. She was almost too good to be true.

"Justin!" Ray said his name in a panic.

He opened his eyes and ran up the stairs. The first he saw outside was Jonah walk up to the front door.

"Shit!" Justin pointed to the floor. "Get down."

Jonah knocked on the front door. Justin stood behind the door and didn't answer.

Lisa walked into People's Park and found the normal crowd. Behind her, the rush-hour of nighttime cruising up and down the strip kept flowing. The front wall was lined with kids, Zoe and the older mix of first-generation punks and hippies sat on the benches at the back of the park. The hole at the center of the park was there; gaping but ignored. Lisa pulled out the make-up mirror she took off of Fred. She angled it to the hole.

The creatures of light were pouring from it. Invisible to the naked eye the beings spilled out by the hundreds every second. She angled the mirror to look at the punks lined up on the wall. They looked human. Lucas and Dave, the singer of the band *With Authority* were the only punks out of high school sitting on the front wall. Lucas was there with his cute little brother who, at twelve years old, was rocking his brother's hand-me-down *Misfits* shirt.

Lisa walked up and sat down next to them. "You guys got minute to talk?"

Lucas lit a cigarette and shook back his long hair. He didn't say yes, but he listened.

"You guys see anything weird, like unexplainable, lately? People being extra assholes?"

Dave laughed. "It's Indiana, it breeds assholes."

Lucas took a drag. "Yeah, can you be more specific?"

Lisa looked at the hole and then back to Lucas. "What if Fred wasn't crazy?"

"I never said he was," Lucas smiled. "He sees the world differently; he is tuned to a different wavelength. It is not his fault."

"He is right about the park," Lisa held up the mirror so he could see the hole. Lucas got wide-eyed as he watched the tiny reflection. The light in the reflection lit up his face. His little brother looked over his shoulder.

"What the fuck?" They said together.

She handed the mirror to Dave. "What am I seeing?"

"We have to fill that fucking hole," Lisa pointed at it.

Traffic stopped on Kirkwood Ave. The world became silent, Lisa looked at her watch and the second hand had stopped ticking. She heard a burst of laughter that shook the sky like thunder. She stood up and it felt as if the gravity had gotten stronger or something was trying to hold her down to the wall.

Time had not slowed. It stopped. The only thing she heard was her own breath. Then, slowly, she heard someone else take long deep breaths in and out. She wanted to ask who was there. She couldn't move her mouth to speak.

There was snap, like a giant thumb and index finger met in the sky. The sound shook creation back to life. Lisa jumped up awkwardly.

"What was that?" Lucas asked. His little brother pointed towards Kirkwood. The cars were still stopped in the street. Their doors opened to unleash what seemed like a wall of big, angry-looking rednecks.

"Well, Dave, here is the war you were expecting."

Dave stood up and cracked his knuckles. Lisa understood what they didn't. They were protecting the hole.

"Come on dude, I know you're there. Let me in. I'm freaked out dude. My mom is gone, I don't know what to do." Jonah begged on the other side of the door. This didn't sound like the angry screaming Jonah they left locked in Fred's bathroom.

Ray and Emily stood around the corner in the kitchen. They both shook their heads "no" at the idea of opening the door. Ray had bruises on his arms from fighting Jonah at Fred's apartment. Justin peaked through the glass from the side window. Jonah looked normal; he wasn't wearing the crazy warrior get up.

"Jonah, was that you at Fred's apartment?"

"What? It wasn't me. I swear I told him no."

Justin leaned on the door. "What do you mean you said no?"

"The other me, the big scary one, offered to put my family back if I stopped Fred."

Ray came up behind Justin. "No, that is not how this works. They are body snatchers, and if you block the frequency, you block them. The rules keep changing."

Jonah pounded on the door. "Fuck the rules!"

Emily nodded. "Ray is right. Horror movies always have rules."

"This isn't a horror movie," Justin yelled so Jonah could hear him through the door. "Reality is broken, there are no rules. Once the walls started coming down...don't you see? Ask Fred."

Emily came up and opened the door. "He's one of us."

"Don't!" Ray put up his fists like an old-time boxer. Jonah stood there, too nervous to come inside. After a few seconds, they all knew he was not the same person they fought at Fred's. Jonah and Justin hugged. They both felt relief, but Ray stood off to the side. He still wasn't sure. Jonah patted his chest.

"It's me, bro," Jonah smiled.

"Oh shit!" Ray pointed out the door. Justin turned to see the Warrior Jonah running toward them with an ax in the air. Behind him was a monstrous version of Ray who had four arms; each holding a blade. A ten-foot-tall version of Justin seemed to command them forward.

Justin slammed the door. "Grab the bats in the garage!" Justin yelled, as a fist came through the narrow window beside the front door. Three bodies pounded away on the door from the outside.

They were a little distracted. Fred engaged his mental cloaking device and tiptoed through the living room. He went out the side door as the kids confronted their demon doppelgangers. He stopped, briefly, to watch the demons banging on the door. They were twisted versions of the boys, and he felt sorry that they had to do battle with themselves. He felt the desire to help them but there was nothing more he could do now that he'd opened their eyes.

Fred ran into the night. He wasn't sure where he was going. The home wasn't safe and the park wasn't safe. They were finally coming to get him.

Fred moved along the sidewalk on the dark street. The streetlights snap crackled and popped but failed to come on, leaving the darkness absolute.

The homes went dark as he passed. It was as if the light was suddenly afraid of him. The only remaining glow came from the road. He stopped to stare at it. It looked as if the road was tiled by giant television screens built into the asphalt, going west all the way down the road. He stepped onto the first screen, tapping the glass with his shoe. The giant screen showed Lisa in the park. She has also faced demons, he thought. But these did not look like archons, they looked like typical people, but Fred knew that simulacra. He was worried about them. He wished they had weapons to fight back with.

Fred walked to the next screen it was also as wide as the road and ten feet tall. This screen showed Justin and his friends in a pitched battle with their evil doppelgangers. Fred shook his head and ran down the road. He stopped on a screen that showed Professor Fred putting a gasmask on his daughter to walk her to school. The next he saw another Fred at a blackboard writing with a thick piece of chalk. He underlined the bold letters. YOU CAN SAVE THEM ALL.

Fred watched the various screens and saw all of reality collide.

CHAPTER TWENTY-TWO

THE CONFRONTATION WAS ALWAYS simmering. The townies were mostly sons and daughters of middle-class professors and teachers. The so-called punks and skaters came from privilege and money. Not all of them, but enough to create a stereotype. The so-called rednecks and jocks grew up in rural little townships around the county that fed into the Bloomington high schools. Some came from neighboring towns like Martinsville to the north where people had little to do outside of high school sports or Klan rallies. More than once students on visiting sports teams from the schools in Indianapolis avoided going to Martinsville after their black athletes were subjected to verbal abuse. Other Cruisers came from the south in Bedford or French Lick, Larry Bird's home town. There was a reason the basketball star was called 'the Hick from French Lick', because small towns like that had so little going on that their teenagers came to Bloomington just to drive up and down Kirkwood.

Lisa never understood the motivation. Show-off their cars, waste gas or pick up chicks? She supposed there were women who were impressed by mullets and muscle cars. Maybe they were impressed when these same guys made jokes mocking skaters and punks. The tension was real at school, and the teachers kept the violence in check. The locals she understood, but if you hated the people that were in the gravity of the university, why come here?

The simple answer was they wanted the conflict. It was only a matter of time before the wrong cruiser and punk crossed paths. So, deep down, everyone was ready for this battle. It would've happened eventually, even without a trans-dimensional alien invasion. Fred called them agents of the void. The human shell was just a costume veiled by a fake reality that she had looked through. They were no longer hiding what they were. They walked toward the park and carried medieval-looking weapons.

"We need something to fight with," Lisa whispered. She looked around and saw the weapons in the hands of the punks around her. It was as if her words brought the swords, battle-axes, and knives into existence. No one holding the weapons seemed surprised. Lisa felt a wave of shock; she didn't have a moment to question it. She raised her sword.

"Attack!" Dave yelled as he lifted his ax into the air. Lisa hung back as the warriors collided. She wanted to scream. The disbelief overwhelming. She looked up and the night sky suddenly burned orange. The hole in the park was now glowing. Lisa watched the glowing light climb up into the sky and gasped.

Clouds flowed from every direction at impossible speed and formed a face. It was Fred's face, and it took up the whole sky above the park. Slowly, it morphed from a sick smile to a face filled with terror. Behind her, she heard the sounds of battle. She couldn't wait for the concrete, she had to fill the hole now. She ran towards it holding the sword high.

"Stop her!" A voice called out.

She turned to see an army of monsters coming after her.

Warrior Jonah's arm busted through the tiny window beside the door frame. He got a grip on Justin. Ray ran up the steps with a baseball bat. Justin felt the bat strike the arm holding him. It was enough to break free. He stepped back and Emily threw him another bat. All three stood in front of the door, bats held high, ready to swing.

Justin had hated Little League two summers earlier but he went because his father wanted him to. He didn't finish the summer out, eventually telling his dad he would rather stay home and read comics. He was glad now that they had so many bats.

"No hiding," Fred's voice from above shook the house like it came from a giant speaker in the sky. Justin looked downstairs. "Make sure Fred is still down there." The creatures on the other side of the door ran full speed and slammed it with terrific force. The door shook in the frame; the deadbolt barely stopping them. Emily came back up the stairs and shook her head.

"He's gone!"

"Fred, where are you?" Justin yelled. He didn't expect an answer.

"This is fucking crazy," Jonah yelled as he held up a comically large kitchen knife that looked like a hatchet.

There was a scream on the other side of the door. Warrior Jonah shoved his long arm through the tiny window. As he screamed, Warrior Jonah pushed himself through the tiny hole like toothpaste coming through a tube. He dripped into the house in sliced parts ripped by the shards of broken glass. As they watched, stunned, the parts began to re-form into Warrior Jonah.

Ray was the first to shake it off. He swung his bat hitting the gooey liquid blob squirming on the floor. He hit it over and over. It was like hitting a puddle. Parts of the monster splashed around the room while other parts of the body were still coming through the window and reforming with the rest.

"Downstairs!" Justin yelled as he pulled on Emily who continued to swing the bat with her free hand. Jonah watched frozen in horror as a nightmare version of him became solid in front of him. The next face to come through the window was Justin's.

"No! We can't run!" Ray yelled as he swung the bat over and over. Warrior Jonah absorbed the blows and laughed. He didn't attack. He just stood there until Ray got tired of hitting him.

It suddenly occurred to Justin, that he only had one bat. Ray took his home before the move. He never had three. All of their bats looked like his black and grey aluminum bat. But Ray's bat, which sat in the garage, had a dark green rubber grip. He wanted desperately for the bats to be there. He convinced himself that the bats were there, and now they were. It was too convenient.

"Lisa needs you!" Fred's voice was so loud Justin felt it in his skull.

Time slowed for a moment. None of this made sense. The warrior monster copies of themselves, the extra bats, Fred's voice. Nothing made sense.

Justin looked at his doppelganger. Jonah fell back on the floor, dropping the knife. Ray stepped back knowing his efforts were useless. Emily gripped her bat, but she already had a foot on the basement steps with Justin. There was nothing left to be done. Justin prayed for it to stop. He directed everything in his mind to the thought, concentrating so hard, he closed his eyes.

There was silence. He opened his eyes and looked into the eyes of the evil Justin. "You're not a body snatcher."

The evil versions of themselves laughed. Justin was confused. "What are you?"

"Don't trust anything, not even what you see," Evil Justin's mouth moved but it was Fred's voice. Evil Justin attacked. Justin closed his eyes again. He just wanted this to end. They needed to close the hole in the park. Nothing else would stop them. They couldn't wait for concrete. Justin felt hands grip his throat.

"Lisa needs you in the park!" Fred's voice shook the house and suddenly all the windows shattered. The hands gripping his neck released. Justin gripped the banister to the stairwell. Jonah and Ray fell into the living room. The house shook violently and then rose. Their stomachs dropped like on a roller coaster. The evil doppelgangers stopped attacking. They only laughed, like banshees, non-stop over and over. The barrier of the windows now gone a storm outside bashed the house. It was as if they were thrown into a hurricane. Wind and rain blew into the house.

Justin heard his friend's screams. The house spun like a top. The furniture slid up and down across the carpet. Framed pictures, plates, seat cushions, and a fireplace stoker all floated in the air. They dodged it all as their screams mixed with the laughter.

The world spun by outside the window. Lightning lit the room as if it was inches away. The clouds cleared for a moment and Justin realized they were spinning high above the city. Outside the windows it looked like they were thousands of feet in the air.

Emily suddenly lifted into the air, pulled towards the windows by the shifting air pressure. Justin held on to the banister and grabbed Emily's hand. He watched the bat slip away and fly out the window with the speed of a bullet. Jonah held on to a chair as he was pulled toward the window.

"No!" Emily reached for him, but the rush of air kept pulling on Jonah. The Monsters had no trouble standing, the rush of air was not even messing with their hair. It was as if they stood outside of the chaos.

Jonah's feet were pulled into the air. In seconds he was gone, sucked out the window. His screams faded as he disappeared into the air below.

"Shit!" Ray jumped too late grasping at the air that had been his friend's ankle. Ray got pulled out of the window and into the storm, too. His screams faded quickly.

Lightning flashed and lit the inside of the house for a few seconds. Justin looked out at the clouds as they swarmed from chaos into a giant eye. Not clouds in the shape of an eye, but a real eye the size of a building. It blinked and Justin noticed it was capped by a gray-haired wild eyebrow line. Justin knew whose giant eye watched him.

Electric Fred.

"Let go, Justin...Let go and I will...take you where you need to go."

The voice boomed, partly in his ears and partly in his mind. He had no choice but to let go. His hand was burning, his muscles were giving way. In the chaos, he looked at Emily. Her long flowing green hair was back. The loving beauty of her eyes grabbed him like a hug. He loved her but had never said those words to anyone but family. He didn't want to let her go, but his strength was giving.

"It's okay, let go," Emily said as she closed her eyes. Justin felt her hand slipping. The wind pulled harder. His hand burned, trying to hold on. "I love you," Emily yelled over the roar.

The words shocked him, and he found he could let go of the banister but not her.

It was instant relief from his hand to his shoulder when he finally let go. The feeling of being weightless for that instant was freedom. Emily didn't scream. She gripped his hand tighter as forces unseen pulled them at unbelievable speed.

He felt the sting of the rain pellets and the whip of the wind. It only lasted an instant.

CHAPTER TWENTY-THREE

The sound of swords clashing was like the crack of thunder. Even the air itself seemed to shake. Lisa stepped back and watched in disbelief as it seemed both sides of the conflict knew how to wield their weapons like experts. Swords slashed and blocked, bodies collided, and the battle raged at the edge of the park. Zoe kept fighting even with a sword buried in his left shoulder. He screamed in pain but kept slashing.

Lisa gripped her sword and turned away from the battle. She felt like she had lived this moment several times before. Again, she ran at the gaping hole with her sword held high.

"Stop her!" She heard a chorus of voices. She turned to look back and prayed this time it didn't happen. The world spun around her. "Fuck! Stop!" She knew without looking that she was back at the front of the park. A sword came down at her in the hands of a giant ogre. She lifted her sword to block and wondered how many times she had repeated this process. She slid the sword into the chest of the giant beast and kicked it back. She looked to her right. Zoe kept fighting even as a sword was buried in his shoulder. He screamed in pain but kept swinging. She turned and ran again toward the hole.

"Stop her!"

This time Lisa stopped five feet from the hole and stabbed her sword into the ground. The world spun around her like a scene inside a snow globe. Unseen forces pulled at her. She held on to the sword; the only thing keeping her from being thrown back into the main battle again. As the sounds of the battle continued behind her, she kept her focus on the hole.

In the steel of her blade, she saw a faint reflection of the beings pouring out of the hole in the ground. "No!" Lisa yelled before looking back. The winged creatures, hoofed ogres, and the various inhuman beings were winning the battle. Her friends were at their feet, covered in blood and gore. The small park was now soaking in the dark red of human blood.

The monsters walked toward her slowly now. Each step shook the ground beneath her and her heart skipped a beat with every step, like a needle bouncing over a scratched record. She turned back to the hole and crawled. The gold light of the beings escaping was no longer hidden. They climbed to the heavens for all the world to see.

Lisa was going to block it, even if she had to use her whole body. She looked through the light and saw the shapes of people at the back of the park. It didn't matter what those shapes were, nothing could stop her now.

Fred stood on the curb watching the massive television screen built into the road in front of him. He saw Lisa crawling towards the hole and the aftermath of the battle at People's Park on one screen. Next to it he watched Justin Morgan's house spin above the city. On a third screen he saw Professor Fred and his family waiting in a long line of people to enter a beam of light. One-by-one, the people in front of them who stepped into the beam disappeared. Inch-by-inch, Professor Fred and his family got closer to the beam.

He felt like one of those people who yelled at the basketball games on TV, as if they could yell through the screen and tell the players what to do.

"Don't trust anything, not even what you see," he yelled at the screen. He was talking to himself. Just because he saw these things on these giant screens didn't mean it was real. It didn't mean his friends were in danger. Not really. They could be sitting around eating chocolate bon-bons, or watching movies, like kids do.

He watched Lisa on one of the screens. She held on to her sword, but the monsters were coming for her. Poor Zoe, Lucas and the others were no match for the creatures. Their bodies lay in heaps at the front of the park. Fred's eyes strayed to the scene in the Morgan house on the next screen. He moved closer to watch. Lisa needed their help.

Fred yelled again. "Lisa needs you in the park!"

Fred had his hands over his mouth. He could hardly watch. Suddenly there was a sound that caught his attention. A loud car engine, mixed with an equally loud guitar and driving beat were coming closer.

The music got even louder and more clear as it approached. "Is there anybody out there? Anybody care?" Fred looked up to see the blue Chevy Nova cruising down the street of TV screens. It looked magical driving over the glow of the television monitors. "Oh, I just gotta know, if you're really there, if you really care."

The muscle car came to a stop in front of Fred, blocking his view of the scenes in the park and the house. The song went to the chorus "Fo-fo-foolin .'" Super-Cruiser leaned down and looked at Fred, who saw himself reflected in the man's glasses. The rock music got softer.

"Move that beast," Fred shouted. "My friends are in terrible danger."

"Tell Justin this," Super-Cruiser spoke carefully. "Let go, Justin. Let go and I will take you where you need to go."

Fred put his hands up. "Why would I?"

"Tell him and get in the car Fred." The door opened on its own.

"Let go, Justin!" Fred shouted. "Let go and I will take you where you need to go."

"See now, was that so fuckin' hard?"

Fred took a seat in the car and crossed his arms in protest. The door squeaked a little as it shut. Super-Cruiser slowly moved them forward.

"Where are you taking me?" Fred asked.

"I should ask you that question?" Super-Cruiser laughed "I just want to talk Fred."

"So, talk." Fred was annoyed. "About what?"

Super-Cruiser pulled off his sunglasses. His eyes glowed with an inhuman glow. "Why the glowing eyes, huh?"

Fred shrugged. "I don't know what you are."

"I'm just a part of you Fred, I am your perception of the real-life Super-Cruiser, but let's face it you don't know my name. Neither do I. I only know what you have absorbed or overheard in the park. That is why I am just your idea of Super-Cruiser. Well, and add a little bit of them boy's perception now, too."

"That's ridiculous," Fred laughed.

"I have glowing eyes and we are driving on a road made of giant TVs showing fragments of your thoughts brought to life on screen. So how ridiculous is it?"

"Bullshit, those boys and the angel..."

"Lisa, her name is Lisa, as she has told you many times."

"OK then Lisa," Fred tapped the window. "They are doing things I couldn't imagine. They listen to music I don't understand. They talk to their parents. I don't know their parents."

"You listen, Fred. I just told ya, They're right here." Super-Cruiser pointed at his temple.

"What? That is impossible."

"What else could explain this?" Super-Cruiser shrugged as he turned the wheel. He was taking them back downtown toward the park.

"It can't happen, it is not possible."

"We ain't gonna explain it Fred. Ain't never gonna have a reason, but you gotta let go of them kids."

Fred thought back to the first time he met them They mocked him in the park. He grabbed Justin. He wasn't sure why he had. Lisa tried to stop him. Ray and Jonah pulled Justin away.

"They need to let go," Fred said softly.

"Do they? You have a lot to let go of buddy."

"If this is true," Fred held up a finger. "Then you are just a figment of my imagination. I am not sure why I should listen to you Mister Cruiser."

Super-Cruiser laughed. "Fred, I understand you have seen some shit. I get it, but if you want to free those kids you have to let go."

"They are holding me!" Fred yelled.

The Chevy Nova pulled into the alley behind the Von Lee theater and drove slowly the last block towards the back of the park. Fred leaned forward in his seat. Justin, Ray, and Jonah were picking themselves off the ground in a grassy patch at the back of the park.

"Tell them where they are Fred," Super-Cruiser whispered.

Fred looked past the boys to the center of the park. The light beings were a flowing geyser rising up from the void. Fred's heart skipped a beat. He felt danger, like it was a pain creeping up his spine. Like it climbed a ladder in his soul.

The agents of the void would say anything to trick him.

Alternate realities, simulations, alien invasions, time-traveling nano-bots, Communist bees, robotic first ladies, telekinetic cats, parrots with mind-controlling parasites, space-traveling ropes and now disillusion. He had written about many other things in his notebook over the years. They tried to convince him not to care, to be apathetic in the face of it all.

Fred turned to Super-Cruiser and his glowing eyes. "Liar!"

CHAPTER TWENTY-FOUR

Justin screamed as soon as he flew out the window. He expected the feeling of the wind, the rain, the sense of falling, but he felt only the grass below his feet. It was a little wet from the summer humidity.

The ground was a welcome shock. He almost kissed the grass. His heart was beating a thousand miles an hour. His breath was labored. He felt a hand on his back and he turned to see Ray, whose hair and clothes were soaking wet. Jonah was wet too.

"I was falling," Ray shook his head. "And then I was here."

"Look!" Jonah pointed.

Justin looked across the park to see the hole spitting the beings of light into the air. Faintly behind the glow, he saw the shape of a thousand evil things. Monsters both winged and horned, muscled and armed, were walking in their direction. Emily stood up and waved them forward. She was already near the light.

Ray helped Justin up. Jonah and Ray stood at the back of the park as Justin ran. When he got to Emily she disappeared. It was like she turned to sand. He was pelted by it as he reached the light. He saw flashes in his mind as the light went through him.

He saw a tortured world with a burnt sky. Tattered flags flew over crumbling cities that were flooded with the blood from all the bodies that were left behind to rot. Their world was choked by industrial madness and governmental insanity. The war machine was only outdone by the forks and shoes that were needed for the multitude of mouths and feet that came into the already overcrowded reality.

Yes, our world was flawed, but compared to the one the creatures were leaving it was pristine. Suddenly, Justin felt a thousand minds try to latch on to his, to take his body. He resisted. Falling to his knees, he dropped his arm into the hole all the way up to his shoulder. Someone else stuck their arm into the whole beside him. It was Lisa.

"Get out of here! I got this," Lisa yelled in his ear. Justin shook his head. Both of their arms fit into the hole, like a perfect puzzle piece. For the moment they blocked the flow of the beings from entering their reality. Justin felt intense pressure from below. It was like his hand was dipped in fire. His mind resisted. He heard a thousand voices scream at him, to pull out, to let them free.

"Don't listen to them," Lisa begged. "They want to steal our world."

They both screamed as the pain grew. Justin looked up to see the monsters coming closer. Ray jumped over him. He punched at the first winged creature who tossed him aside. Justin heard Jonah shouting but he knew it was over. The monsters would uncork them and the battle would soon be lost.

Fred watched it unfold from the passenger seat of the Chevy Nova. Lisa and Justin bravely plugged the hole, and for a brief moment, the flow of void agents stopped. Fred leaned back in the seat.

"Oh no, you don't get to relax now Fred," Super Cruiser was angry.

"I have listened to enough of your lies."

"My lies, your lies. I am you, Fred. The winged monsters are you. The light beings are just your mind trying to make sense of it all, going back to the day this park was created."

"Shut up," Fred looked away.

"Every moment you let this go on you allow their minds to be tortured. They may never recover. You know what that means."

"I said shut up!"

Super-Cruiser punched the steering wheel. "You have to do this Fred. You know this place, this little parking lot-sized park that became home to these freaks and weirdos, would not be here without that first act of violence. There would be some kind of a store or a restaurant, like the rest of the places along this strip."

"I said enough!"

"This home away from home has hate dripping in the soil."

"Yes, it does! It should never have existed."

Super Cruiser tapped on the window. "It did need to happen. The community came together and demanded a park, and now instead of being a burger joint or a bar, it is a beautiful space. The bombing was awful, but the seeds of hate didn't grow, Fred. You are a part of it, Fred. Sure, they might make jokes, but you are a part of the fabric of this place. Not crazy, not insane but outside of the mainstream; a voice of the other worlds that exist beyond what they can see."

Fred looked at Lisa and Justin screaming as they blocked the hole in the center of the park.

"They're dying," Fred whispered.

"No, they think they are dying. Fred, buddy old pal. Go tell them to let go or they will lose their minds forever."

Fred thought of the hours he spent in therapy, the walls at the hospital, the hours spent writing in the notebooks and the subtle pain he felt being misunderstood. He couldn't let that happen to the angel and those boys.

"What can I do?" Fred whispered.

Super Cruiser smiled. "I thought you'd never ask. All you gotta do is ask them nicely to get out of your mind. Set them free."

CHAPTER TWENTY-FIVE

Lisa ignored the pain as she did when she got her first tattoo. Her mother told her she had ruined her life over a Kali tat that could always stay hidden under her sleeve. It was the latest in a lifetime of fights over how she chose to live her life. Her mother had lived on the south side of Indianapolis her whole life. Her idea of an exotic vacation was the speed boat regatta in Madison on the Ohio River. They had different ideas about what was style and culture when Lisa was younger.

Her mother never wanted to be seen or noticed. She thought the goth lifestyle was ugly and a desperate cry for attention. They fought over it most days. Her father had no energy to engage. He didn't like it and thought it looked silly, but he also didn't care. Once he got home from the lumber yard, he barely had the energy to open a beer and catch the Pacers game. When Lisa got accepted to IU, she was told there was no money. She had to do it all on her own.

Lisa closed her eyes and came to a feeling of peace with the pain. She didn't know how it all got to this point; why it was her that had to sacrifice herself.

"Justin, get out of here." She managed to say

He just grunted. The way they blocked the hole she was looking at the back of the park and he faced the front.

"What are they doing?" She asked. He didn't answer, she felt his body shaking, and she knew the pain he was in.

She blinked twice, not sure if what she saw was in her imagination. That blue Chevy Nova driven by the guy everyone called Super Cruiser was stopped in the Alley behind the park. The door opened and Fred stepped out. He walked toward them holding a notebook and a pen. One of the winged creatures screamed and flew over her towards Fred.

"Run, Fred!"

Like a bird of prey, the grey-skinned monster dived at Fred who didn't flinch. At the last second, he smacked it with a notebook. The creature spun out on the ground before turning to dust.

The tree at the back of the park that had grown mighty in the short time since the park was founded twisted as it came to life. Fred looked at the tree and smiled. The branches formed a hand and reached for him.

Fred turned to face the tree as it twisted into a creature. "No! I know better!"

Lisa blinked and the tree was normal again.

"Ha!" Fred walked toward them and the sounds of battle behind them disappeared as if the volume was turned down. Lisa looked straight up and saw the monsters that Fred called Agents of the Void frozen in place. The burning sensation in the hole stopped. Lisa let her body relax but kept blocking the hole.

"What the fuck is happening?" She heard Ray behind her.

"Fred did it!" Jonah yelled.

"Justin, are you okay?" Emily begged.

"It stopped, all of it." Justin sounded ready to cry.

Fred leaned down towards Lisa. He smiled and made eye contact with her. In all the times they talked he never looked directly at her. "You can get up now Lisa," Fred said.

Lisa was shocked. Fred never remembered or seemed to know her name. He called her angel or a dozen incorrect names.

Lisa used her free arm to push herself up. Fred helped her up. She looked around. The monsters were frozen in place. Her second hand on her watch had stopped moving. Emily and Ray helped Justin to stand.

Fred smiled. Lisa turned and looked back down in the hole. She knelt down and put her whole face in it and saw the flip side. It was the same park, but the buildings on the other side were in ruins. There was a single-file line of people waiting to jump into the hole.

"Why did they stop?" Lisa sat back up. The boys and Emily sat down next to them on the grass. Fred set his notebook down. He thumbed through the pages. Finally, he opened to the handwritten page he wanted. He pointed to the word on the page and started reading:

"I would use any deity to further the cause of people. Human civilization is my main love. I would share the magic with everyone. Oh, you need magic so bad, the magic pen writes you in. It writes you out. You have to let go, you understand, when the moment is here. You must let go."

"Fred, what do you mean by..." Lisa felt a wind brush by as the world spun. In a moment all the monsters were gone. Even the night washed away into blinding daylight. Lisa had to close her eyes against the sudden brightness. The park began to spin.

Fred sat in the middle of the park. He was the only thing that didn't move. He was the metal rod at the center of a turntable. Ray reached out to grab Jonah who grabbed Justin, who grabbed Lisa, and she grabbed onto Fred's leg. Like a human chain connected to Fred, they held on as the park spun faster.

"Where's Emily?" Justin shouted over the roar of the spinning park. Lisa looked back but didn't see the young woman. The world beyond the park disappeared. Lisa screamed.

CHAPTER TWENTY-SIX

Justin held on to Jonah with one hand and Lisa with the other. Her screams echoed in an unnatural way. He couldn't see Emily. Not only was Emily missing, but the world beyond the park had disappeared.

"Where is Emily?" He yelled but no one answered. Justin let go, Ray and Jonah tumbled around before Ray grabbed the metal legs of a bench with one hand and struggled to hold on to Jonah with the other. Justin rolled around on the surface of the park. He tried to stand but imagined it was like trying to stand on the surface of a spinning LP. He tumbled to the front and only stopped when he hit the stone wall at the front of the park where the punks hung out.

"Emily!" Justin lifted himself up to the top of the short wall. Faintly, he heard his friends calling his name. Once over the wall he looked out and where the sidewalk should have been he saw only stars. He hugged the wall tighter as he stared out into what seemed to be outer space. One star in the sky flared brighter than the others before it disappeared.

Suddenly, the massive view across the sky above him changed into the eye piece of a large telescope. A young woman stood smiling beside it, holding a notebook.

Catherine. Something told him her name.

"That's three we can mark off our list. How about a beer?"

The sky flashed. Now he saw Kirkwood Ave. It was a cold night. Slush lined the gutters and the sidewalks were covered in snow that had turned gray. The sudden shift to winter was not the only change. It didn't look right. The street lamps were different. The cars on the streets looked older. Only the Von Lee Theater looked the same. He saw Catherine, the woman from the telescope, walking with a young man. It took Justin a moment to realize it was a younger Fred.

A car stopped in front of Justin. He knew what he was watching as the man got out of the car. He wanted to shout no! He felt it as if it was a memory, but it wasn't his own.

"Go back to Africa, n*****s!" The man yelled. Justin closed his eyes before the flaming bottle came towards him. Justin felt the heat of the fire whizz by him. It was a relief from the cold night air around him. He heard the bottle crash; felt the flames. He saw Fred standing just beyond fire, his eyes only reflecting the horror.

Suddenly, Justin's view shifted to the inside of an apartment. The image of it took up the entire sky beyond the park. Catherine was a few years older. her hair cut shorter. She was packing her clothes in a suitcase. She had been crying and didn't try to hide it. She sobbed openly as she zipped up the suitcase. Fred was busy writing in his notebook.

"Bye Catherine, I'll miss you, Catherine." She said with sarcasm, but Fred never looked up. Justin was not sure he even heard her.

Lightning flashed, and a new scene appeared. The image zoomed over a forest. Justin felt the warm wind of a summer day. The image of the flight continued through a building that was almost entirely one massive computer. At the center of it was Fred sitting at a keyboard typing. It was a very different looking Fred, wearing shades and a trench coat. It wasn't possible, but it felt like a memory, too. He remembered finding the code, the zeroes and ones which were the spine of the universe.

Over and over the sky flashed and another scene involving Fred loomed in the sky. He saw Fred reject the simulation theory, Fred traveling space by rope, calculating the distance between stars and making french toast for Catherine and their daughter in another world and Catherine dying in his arms, an old woman, Catherine losing her mind, Fred leaving her.

He saw the pages of notebook after notebook flash before his eyes. Faintly, against a backdrop that looked like a vast nebula that was close enough to reach out and touch. The pages kept flipping by against this glorious array of stars.

Justin turned back to see his Fred and his friends. The spin of the park was slowing down. The slower the pages turned, the slower the park spun.

"Holy shit, you guys gotta see the crazy shit he is writing in his notebook." A voice echoed in the sky.

Justin walked back towards Fred. Ray and Jonah stood up. They were looking up listening to the voice. They knew it was Jonah's voice.

"Hey back off you little shits, leave Fred alone."

"Wait this guy is Electric Fred."

They all looked up and saw themselves in a chain connected to Fred. *"I feel your anger. Oh sure this space was intended for community, but now it is anger and hate that opens us up."*

Fred snapped his notebook. The ground shook, everything in the sky disappeared as if the park was out of space and time. Justin, Ray and Jonah stood over Fred. Lisa still held on to him.

"What happened?" Lisa asked.

Fred looked away. "It is my fault. I have tried to understand it, but I can't explain it. You see that was my mistake trying to explain it."

"Explain what?" Justin sat down in front of Fred.

Fred looked at him this time. "All of it. Why would God gave me the ability to reason but not give the same ability to a bee or slug? Why a universe so vast and amazing would give these wonderful gifts to one species bent on self-destruction is impossible to explain. Sometimes, I believe it is God. Sometimes, I think it must be a code written by someone with a sick sense of humor."

"You don't have to know everything Fred," Lisa rubbed his shoulder.

"Where were you angel, when I needed those words? You see I needed to explain how someone could be so Goddamn intolerant? I needed to understand why people don't see the world the way I do." Fred sighed. "I don't know why you are here. I think the universe wanted you to see creation through my eyes."

Justin shook his head. "All this?"

Lisa smiled. "It isn't real, it is just perception. Fred's perception."

"So, my family is still okay, they are still normal...?"

"Yeah," Lisa smiled. "Back in reality. You see, Fred's perception joined yours. We are in his mind."

"Sorry," Fred shrugged. "It is your perception and mine, mixed together like a cake mix.."

"No offense," Ray shrugged. "But how the fuck do we get out of it?"

"We have to let go, back at the park." Lisa tapped the ground, or what appeared to be ground. "That first moment when Fred gabbed you, and I grabbed him."

"I grabbed you," Ray pointed at Justin.

"I was holding on too," Jonah added.

Justin put up his hands. "What about Emily?"

No one answered his question.

"I'm letting go," Jonah opened his hand, even though the act was in his mind. In seconds his body shimmered and disappeared.

"That simple," Ray smiled before he disappeared. The feeling of a grip on Justin's arm appeared and disappeared in the same instant. Lisa and Fred watched him.

Justin felt an unexpected sorrow. Despite all the scary things he had seen in the last few days there was one undeniably beautiful thing; one person that he got weak kneed just thinking about.

"So, she was never really here?"

Lisa nodded. "I'm sorry."

"I thought she loved me."

"It is something we all hold on to," Fred sounded amazingly clear. "We think he or she is the one. But, 'the one' is rarely the first one."

"What if I want to stay here Fred? Can't I just stay here?" It was tempting for him to live in a reality that bent to his perception. The problem is, he knew, you can also become the victim of it.

Fred pointed at his temple and shook his head. "You can't stay here. I'm letting go Justin."

Justin had the feeling of falling. He reached out, trying to hold on to Lisa but she was already gone.

CHAPTER TWENTY-SEVEN

IT WAS THE FEELING of gravity that surprised him. Time slowed and stretched, yet he felt stars ignite and die. Justin felt the world sprouting with life and dying a cold death in the void. He opened his eyes and saw Lisa let go of Fred. She almost fell over.

Fred fell back on the bench next to his open notebook, exhausted. Justin reached up. His mohawk was gone.

Justin turned around and saw his cousin Smiley. Lucas, the taller long-haired punk rocker was in his face. "Leave Fred alone man, he never harmed anyone."

"Fuck with Fred, you fuck with me," said Zoe, fresh off a swig of a bottle in a bag.

Smiley put up his hands. "I ain't fuckin with your hippie friend."

"Hey Smiley," Justin got his cousin's attention. "Why don't you shut the fuck up?"

A punk dude with a mustache was passing out blue pieces of paper. Justin took one from him. It was a flyer for a show at the Savage House. He already had one in his pocket. A part of him remembered being at that show. The loud amps, the sweat-covered bodies, the aggression of the slam dancing and – his heart dropped -the feeling of holding Emily's hand.

"That's a mind fuck." He couldn't wrap his head around the idea that the show had not happened yet.

Justin watched Lisa who was wearing the same *Sisters of Mercy* shirt she had on the first day they met. He reminded himself, as hard as it was to believe, it was still that day. She held Fred's hand. He looked like he had just finished a marathon, covered in sweat. He took deep breaths, then looked up at the sky for a long moment and then back at Lisa.

Fred finally managed to smile. "It's over angel. I let go, I promise."

"How did that happen?" Ray whispered. Fred just shook his head. He had no answers to offer.

"It doesn't matter now," Lisa said as she picked up Fred's notebook. "Come on Fred, let's go to the Spoon."

Justin heard a familiar sound, the honk of his mother's horn. "Shit," Justin looked up and saw his mother's car in the alley. Busted! He felt like there was a spotlight on him. Not only were they not where they were supposed to be, but now the whole park, all the punks and weirdos, would see his mom pick them up.

"Hey Mrs. Morgan," Jonah was the first to the car.

Smiley ran up next. "Hey Auntie Nikki, the movie sucked ass."

"Hey language," She waved at her son to follow. Justin hesitated.

"Can we talk about what happened?" Justin asked Lisa.

She helped Fred to his feet. "I don't know Justin. Might be best to..."

"Let go?" He smiled.

Lisa smiled. "I'll see you at the Savage House show maybe?"

Justin looked at the flyer. He loved the memory he had of being there, even if it wasn't real. "Yeah, I mean, fuck yeah, I'll be there."

Justin turned around to take a last look at the park. His heart dropped. There she was. Her hair was totally blond, not dyed green, but it was Emily. Justin put his hand up to wave at her, but she just walked past with her friends and never even looked up at him.

Smiley laughed from the back seat. Justin moped back to the car. He stuffed in beside Ray and Jonah. They were at a loss for words.

Nicole Morgan didn't drive away. She kept the car in park, and turned to look at her son. He felt eyes from all over the park watching them.

"Something tells me you kids didn't see Karate Kid III?"

"Just...I want to go home, Mom."

She turned around and drove. "Some interesting people you were hanging out with."

Lisa helped Fred walk for a bit, but by the time they made it up the steps at the Spoon, he was walking fine on his own. When he sat down, she asked him if he needed his cheese sandwich and coke. He pulled a fresh notebook from his backpack and opened it to the last page. He pointed his pen at the counter and the kitchen. He smiled.

Ursula was counting cash behind the counter when Lisa walked by. "You're five minutes late sweetheart."

Lisa looked up at the clock and the second hand clicked around the clock like heavy footprints. There was a calendar on the wall. She looked at the date and had a strong feeling of vertigo. "It is Saturday...it is Saturday," she whispered to herself.

"You okay, sweetie?" Ursula asked.

She nodded and put together Fred's sandwich. After she grabbed the coke from the cooler she walked over to his table and sat it down. He was busy writing already. He didn't look up. She stood there for a moment and read over his shoulder:

> "You ought to read this. This is interesting. I talk to videotape, and it listens. A Pleiadian from Andromeda comes strolling into view. A dork. He addresses the By-standers "One step forward!" (two steps back)

> "I'm investing in postage for mass distribution of magic. I'm sending every minister of healing a magic wand. Via the postal service. A million dollars will give me good coverage. A million

dollars in postage for working copies of magic devices across the land."

Lisa rubbed Fred's shoulder. "Eat your dinner, Fred." He kept writing.

CHAPTER TWENTY-EIGHT

Nicole Morgan walked into her son's bathroom, as always, fearing the worst. He and his friends never put the seat down, and they left it disgusting. She sighed heavily, finding hair in the sink. It had been a year since the first time he cut his hair into a mohawk, and she still was not used to it. She wanted him to express himself, but could he at least clean up after himself when he did?

She picked up a trash can and found some of Jonah's hair mixed in. It made her laugh. She heard his bedroom door open. Justin wandered out and was surprised to see his mother standing between him and the toilet.

"It's almost 10 am," she said.

Justin pushed past her. "Summer break. We had band practice last night."

"Jonah's mom asked if you guys could practice here, I think Miss Patrick would have a heart attack. I told her no."

Justin peed right in front of his mother. She dropped the hair back in the sink. "And clean up after yourself."

Nicole found Jonah in the kitchen eating cereal. She thought about as saying, "make yourself at home," but they were way past that.

Justin came downstairs and went straight for a bowl. Jonah was in a leather jacket despite the summer heat outside. Her son wore a *Dead Kennedys* shirt; a band name that she didn't find amusing.

She sat at the table next to Jonah so she could sit across from her son. His wild punk look was contrasted by the natural acne that most teenagers fought. He was a handsome boy, and she saw his father in him. She didn't understand how he saw the world, but what parents understood the next generation?

"You guys come up with a band name yet?"

Their first time playing live was only two days away. She knew they put some random name on the flyers with the plan to announce the real name at the show.

"Blood Farts," Jonah smiled. Justin kicked him under the table.

They all laughed. "That is disgusting," she said, "and how did you think I would not find out?"

Justin shrugged. Nicole hated many of the things her son was into. The fights at school, the music, and the hair cut took getting used to. That said, he was smart, and opinionated and she loved that he still liked science fiction just like his dad. Eventually, the comic books faded away and his allowance got spent on punk CDs and LPs. She even bought him a bass guitar and he found someone to teach him.

When he finished his cereal, he almost left his bowl on the table. At the last second, he grabbed it and put it in the sink. He and Jonah had their skateboards in a matter of moments.

"Where you off to?"

"Spaceport!" Jonah yelled. "Record store and the park," Justin said.

Jonah jumped on his skateboard and headed down the hill toward the park. Justin made his way to Karma Records. He had enough money for something used, but more importantly, he had to talk to Whittaker about bass lessons. He was having trouble getting the pace right for one of the *Black Flag* songs that Jonah wanted to play.

He opened the door and waved at Whittaker behind the counter. He was about to say hi when he saw something that took his breath away. She was standing in front of the punk and hardcore singles, flipping through the records.

She was a year older, her hair was cut in a shorter bob, and was dyed the color of pink cotton candy. Justin walked slowly up to the records. He wasn't even going to pretend to look. He wanted so badly to hug her, but she never knew him the way he remembered her. It never happened, but it still felt real to him.

"Emily McRoberts?"

She turned and looked at him. He could see on her face she had to think about who he was. She looked him up and down and her eyes stopped at the band stickers on his skateboard. "Ahh, Justin Morgan, right?"

"Yeah, we were neighbors before I moved... you moved." He nervously laughed. "We moved."

"You stayed in town, right?" She turned back to look at records.

"Yeah, I thought you moved to Cali?"

"I did, I'm just visiting one of my best friends. I like California but I miss my friends."

"I bet."

"Tell her about your show dumbass," Whittaker said as he dropped the needle on a record by *The Accused*. Justin could've been embarrassed, but he pulled out the flyer he had in his pocket.

"We're playing the street dance with *The Walking Ruins* and *With Authority*. It's our first show, so we're opening up."

She smiled. "We were already going, so I suppose I'll see you there." She took three records to the counter and Justin couldn't move. He listened to the sound of her checking out and the door opening. When he knew she was gone he walked to the counter. Whittaker had a goofy smile on his face.

"She was 'the one,' right?"

Justin smiled. "The one."

The street dance was a unique Bloomington thing. One of the local student-run radio stations, WQAX, whose signal didn't reach the outskirts of town, put it on. In the early days, the plan was to have the bands play in the basement of the house they broadcasted from. The problem was, every inch was filled with records of every genre. The DJs were volunteers, and in the last couple of months, from 7pm to 9pm on Wednesdays was the QAX Punk Corner with Jonah.

In the summer, QAX sponsored a show with three bands that would set up on the street hooked up to a generator and play right there on the concrete. Kids would slam dance, the locals would drive by looking confused, and new people wandered into a musical world they didn't know existed.

Justin held his bass and looked out at the sea of people, most of whom were there to see *The Ruins* and *With Authority*, or were just curious to see what these little kids could do.

Jonah had a handwritten set-list on the back of the flyer for the show taped to the pavement in front of him. The night was hot. Before they played a note the whole crowd was already sweating.

Whittaker leaned up against a car and gave Justing a thumbs up. Lisa from the Spoon showed up and she smiled at him. They talked at the park sometimes, but it was weird. She was older and in college. It was odd hanging out with a freshman in high school. They also didn't know how to talk about their experience with Fred.

Ray was nervous behind the drum set. He didn't want to be a drummer but no one else stepped forward. His parents agreed to buy it if it stayed in the band's garage space at Jonah's house. Robert was the best player in the band, inheriting the talent passed down from his parents.

Jonah waited for the guy at the soundboard to give them a thumbs up. "We're *The Blood Farts*, fucking go!"

Justin closed his eyes and launched into the song. He felt the beat. The guitars sounded a million miles away. It was weird not playing in the garage and blasting punk rock into the open Indiana summer night. No one moved or slammed like he imagined they would when they played the song. This was why they put a cover song second in the setlist, based on Whittaker's advice.

The song was just over a minute, and it was his turn to play. Ray started the beat as Justin played the opening bass line to "London Dudgeon" by *The Misfits*. Robert's guitar screamed with feedback. By the time Jonah yelled, "They call us walking corpses, unholy living dead..." the crowd had swelled in. When Justin looked up, he saw faces he knew from school and the park stomping and slamming into each other. He heard the crowd singing louder than Jonah.

Someone bumped into him. He almost dropped his pick, he missed the beat, he screwed up the song for a second while he pushed the person back into the pit. There was no way to explain the power he felt with the song coming through his fingers and plugging into the song. He was connected to the crowd, to his tribe.

The song ended and he wanted to play it again. The same song again, he wanted nothing more than to feel that song again. He was scared that their next song might not carry the crowd. Ray didn't give them time to second guess, he clicked his drumsticks four times and away they blasted into another fast song.

The circle pit was a tornado behind him. Justin couldn't hear the guitar at all, so he looked back at Ray. In the distance, he saw someone about to cross the street. Justin could tell him from a mile away: Electric Fred.

The slam pit swelled forward and knocked Justin into the drum set, knocking over a cymbal. Ray kept playing as Justin set the cymbal straight. Some musicians would be pissed, but Justin loved it. When the song was over, he looked down the street and Fred was gone.

Justin looked out at three generations of Bloomington weirdos. United by the crazy music and the park that had been their home away from home. Fred would never be forgotten by any of them. Justin wished he could thank him for his new view of the universe.

Justin stepped up to Jonah and pointed to his microphone. He took in his hand. "Hey, uh, I want to dedicate this next one to Electric Fred." The crowd cheered. "Wherever you are Fred you'll never be forgotten."

The End.

ACKNOWLEDGMENTS

First and foremost, my partner and best friend Cari, who saved two of Fred's Notebooks: you are always supportive, and the fact that you had those blew my mind.

Langhorne J Tweed for being MVP friend and supporter.

Desmond Reddick and James Chambers who read an early draft and assured me the novel worked for people who had never been to Bloomington.

Keith Giles for believing in the book and getting it.

Also Matthew at Quoir, Susan for hosting us for the release party, John Shirley, Cody Goodfellow, Anthony Trevino, SD HWA, D. Harlan Wilson, Zack Wood, Christoph and Leeza at Clash, Greg at Artifact books, Rob Mysterious Galaxy, Issa Diao, Burn it Downey, Laina, Kevin Burd, Austin Lucas, Bryan Pease, basketball friends in OB, and I missed a bunch of people. Shit. I tried.

ABOUT THE AUTHOR

David Agranoff Grew up in Bloomington, Indiana, hanging in the park that inspired this novel. His future wife worked at the Spoon, serving the real-life Electric Fred. They have two of his notebooks and a house full of rescued animals. David is a novelist, screenwriter, and a Horror and Science Fiction critic. He is the Splatterpunk and Wonderland book award nominated author of 11 books, including the WWII Vampire novel, *The Last Night to Kill Nazis*, the science-fiction novel, *Goddamn Killing Machines* (from CLASH BOOKS), and the Cli-fi novel *Ring of Fire, Punk Rock Ghost Story*. He co-wrote a novel, *Nightmare City* (with Anthony Trevino) that he likes to pitch as "The Wire, if Clive Barker and Philip K Dick were on the writing staff." As a critic he has written more than a thousand book reviews on his blog *Postcards from a Dying World,* which has recently become a podcast, featuring interviews with award-winning and bestselling authors such as Stephen Graham Jones, Paul Tremblay, Alma Katsu, and Josh Malerman. For the last five years, David has co-hosted the *Dickheads Podcast*, a deep-dive into the work of Philip K. Dick—reviewing his novels in publication order, as well as the history of Science Fiction. David's non-fiction essays have appeared on Tor.com, NeoText, and Cemetery Dance. He just finished writing a book, *Unfinished PKD,* on the unpublished fragments and outlines of Philip K. Dick. He lives in San Diego where you can find him hooping in pick-up games and taking too many threes.

To contact David Agranoff for speaking engagements, please visit davidagranoff.blogspot.com or @dagranoffauthor on X.

QUOIR

Many Voices. One Message.

quoir.com.